From Coffee to Chaos

a novel

Todd H. Davis

From Coffee to Chaos
Copyright © 2026 by Todd H. Davis

Name: Davis, Todd H. (1963)
Title: From Coffee to Chaos / Todd H. Davis

Summary: "A young accountant invites a young single mother of three to live with him in exchange for housework, not realizing she would be convicted of theft and sentenced to 28 days in jail. Over campouts, parenting classes, and holiday dinners, the young man and woman begin to appreciate each other and learn what home really means." Author

ISBN: 979-8-9905056-4-3 paperback
               979-8-9905056-5-0 hardcover

Subject: Chosen family; [BISAC: 1. Fiction / Romance / Contemporary 2. Fiction / Romance / Clean & Wholesome 3. Fiction / Family Life / General]

Independently published, Cypress, Texas, USA
For information, contact www.toddhdavis.com
Cover design by Todd H. Davis

From Coffee to Chaos

a novel

Todd H. Davis

Books by Todd H. Davis

CHAPTER 1

Joe

I watched the woman enter the coffee shop, looking harried with three kids in tow. With her multiple facial piercings and neck tattoo, she blended in better among the baristas than among customers. The neck design involved a large lotus flower inked across her throat, sitting atop two rows of lotus petals stretching in a semicircle across her collarbone, easy to view over her wide-neck floral blouse.

As the woman turned to scan the room, I noticed her sleeve tattoo, a design that reminded me of a fir tree branch, complete with Christmas ornaments. Only on her right arm. Her left arm was devoid of ink. I briefly wondered if her jeans hid other artwork. I glanced down to see that a small tattoo of a pair of red slippers reminiscent of Dorothy's red slippers from The Wizard of Oz adorned her right ankle. Surprisingly, at least to me, her hair, which cascaded down past her shoulders, remained naturally brown and not green, blue, or pink.

The time on my phone showed ten past the hour. Audrey was late. I would have waited outside, but the afternoon sun beat down on the storefront, making the already hot day seem hotter. So, I'd done the rude thing of taking a table before placing an order at the counter. Ordering before sitting was an option to prove I belonged, but I hated when movie characters did that. Hollywood seemed to think it was normal that the first to arrive at a restaurant would proceed to get a table and order a drink rather than wait by the entrance for their date.

Not that this counted as a date, but I didn't want Audrey to arrive and find me already nursing an iced latte.

It had been nearly nine years since I'd seen her. After she broke up with me shortly after our high school graduation, I spent the rest of the summer wondering what I did wrong and then trying to forget her. We'd been together for two years. That included two homecomings, two Christmases, and one prom. I thought we were going to the same college, but she didn't show up.

"It's not you," she told me the night she dumped me. "I just need to find myself, to find out who I really am." Yeah, right. Although it was painful, I chose to respect her need for space. I refrained from calling, texting, or driving by her house. But after no contact for the whole summer, I couldn't stand it any longer and called.

No answer. I found out from one of her friends that she'd gone to Europe. Such a trip couldn't have been an impulse decision. She had to have planned it for months. Yet she hadn't even mentioned it before the breakup, which left me feeling betrayed. How long had she planned our breakup? Before prom?

Then, two days ago, she texted, "Hey Joe! I'm back in town. Let's catch up."

I almost ignored it. Over the years, I'd heard rumors through friends of friends, stories of partying and hookups, both in Europe and here in the States. She was no longer the person I knew and loved. By the time I finished college, she was but a distant memory.

I'd dated over the years and was even once engaged. Broke up with my last girlfriend shortly after buying my house last fall. She was upset I hadn't taken her advice on the final purchase. We'd been dating for a few months at the time and were getting closer, but not to the point of planning major purchases together. It was my house, after all, not *our* house. After a few arguments, we both concluded we weren't right for each other. And neither of us had to go to Europe to figure that out.

A few hours after Audrey's text, my curiosity got the better of me. I replied, "How about coffee?" A coffee date – if it was a date – could be as short or as long as you like, safe for an uncertain meetup.

A familiar voice called my name, breaking me out of my reverie, and I stood to look past the tattooed and accessorized mother for Audrey. As I leaned my head to see around the woman, she stepped closer as if intent on blocking my view.

"Joe! It's good to see you!"

It took a moment for my brain to register that the greeting came from the tattooed woman.

"My mother was supposed to watch the kids, but she bailed on me," she explained. Kids, as in, *her* kids.

I felt a little scrape against my cheek as she pressed her face to mine in a hug. "I missed you," she said.

"Good to see you, too," I lied, declining to acknowledge her statement of missing me. I regretted the meetup already. After she released me, I noticed the accessories on each of her cheeks were little pointed studs that protruded from her dimples like silver thorns.

She sat the kids down at the next table, pulled three juice boxes from a Walmart bag, and placed one in front of each kid.

"Mommy!" the middle child, a boy who appeared to be five or six, whined. "Why can't we get something from here?"

The boy wore light blue shorts, a faded dark blue Houston Astros T-shirt, and mismatched socks, one black, one white, protruding from well-worn sneakers. His older brother seemed better dressed. His shirt was a little less faded, his socks matched, and his shoes were less scuffed.

"Babe, we discussed this in the car. They don't have the kind of drinks you like. That's why we brought juice boxes."

The boy looked to his older brother as if seeking support for his plea. The older boy, perhaps seven or eight, simply shrugged his shoulders and produced a tiny toy car from a pocket, placed it on the table, and flicked it with a finger to send it rolling toward his little sister on the other side. Her little legs protruding from her yellow dress ended in white sandals, no socks to mismatch.

After placing the coffee order for us adults at the counter, I observed Audrey and her kids from the safety of the pickup counter. The older boy showed his younger siblings how to tear off the end of a straw wrapper and blow into the straw to send the remaining wrapper flying across the table and into the lap of a young woman, or possibly a teenager, who seemed oblivious to its arrival as she scrolled through her phone.

I took a deep breath and let it out slowly. *What the hell happened to you, Audrey?*

* * *

I started the engine of my Toyota Camry and said, "Call Griffin."

Griffin picked up as I pulled onto the street.

"So?" he asked. "Is she still hot?"

"Not even lukewarm," I told him. "Besides, back then, I didn't think of her as hot; I thought of her as adorably cute. But you were right."

"Which part?"

"She's ready to get serious and settle down."

"I knew it!" he shouted triumphantly. "Was it as bad as we thought?"

"Worse," I said. "Three kids. Different fathers. Lost her job and moved back in with her mom.

"Fat and ugly?"

"A little thicker than she was back in high school, but I wouldn't call her fat. It was hard to get past the neck tattoo and multiple piercings, though. Every time I looked at her nose ring,…"

"Bull or boogers," Griffin interrupted.

"Boogers."

We'd discussed nose rings long before Audrey contacted me. I'm not a fan of piercings at all, other than ears, and I can tolerate a dainty nose stud or thin nostril ring. I drew the line at the septum variety. The ones with the ball ends hanging down remind me of boogers. Those with the loop hanging down remind me of the rings on bulls' snouts.

"And the ring thing on her lip reminded me of a cold sore," I told Griffin.

"So, boogers and cold sores," he summarized.

Moving on from her looks, I said, "She's been living with her mom for the last few months."

"Money problems," he guessed. "How'd you leave things?"

"Not good. When we got around to talking about me, she asked if I was seeing anyone."

"She's interested," he teased.

"I almost made up a fake girlfriend just for the occasion. But I admitted I didn't have anyone. She pointed out she didn't either, which was already pretty clear."

"Run, Dude! Run as fast as you can!"

"Then she said she heard I bought a house, and she's never met anyone our age who already has a house. She admires my success."

"And she's ready to settle down...," he teased again.

I sighed at how well his prophetic prediction came true, then continued. "When she asked to see the house, I made up an excuse and left. Didn't even respond to her request. I wasn't trying to be rude, but her kids were throwing sugar packets around, and I have no desire to see them or her again."

Griffin laughed at my discomfort. "You dodged a bullet back then, and you dodged another one today."

CHAPTER 2

Audrey

I watched him leave and muttered, "Oh, *Helsinki*," as I had run out of both patience and actual swear words. Then I gathered the juice boxes, crumpled napkins, and sugar packets my boys had used for table-soccer championships, shoved the debris into their hands, and pointed them toward the trash. My kids probably think I'm the drill sergeant of cleanliness.

I wanted to cry and scream at the same time – not necessarily *at* Joe, and not even with real words. Maybe just a long, dramatic "WHYYYY." But I was in mom mode, so I swallowed the meltdown, clenched my jaw, and herded my children toward the door.

"Is your friend sick?" Royce asked as we stepped outside.

"Why do you think that?" I asked.

"Because he looked like he had a tummy ache when he left."

"He should eat a cracker," Simone announced with the confidence of a four-year-old who believes saltines can cure emotional trauma.

"I don't think he has a tummy ache," I said. "I think he just doesn't like me."

Colton chimed in, "Then he's an *Oslo*."

My mother had lectured me about cussing like a sailor, so I'd started substituting place names for my favorite expletives. Unfortunately, the kids had adopted the system. *Oslo* was my stand-in for… well, people can probably guess.

"Why doesn't he like you?" Royce asked.

"Because I hurt his feelings a long time ago."

Colton crossed his arms and declared, "He needs to get over it." Which is exactly the kind of thing my mother would say, but minus her judgmental eyebrow.

I unlocked the ancient Dodge Grand Caravan – may it rest in pieces someday – and slid open the side door. Royce buckled Simone into her booster seat while I helped Colton with his. Technically, Royce should've been in a booster too, but when Simone outgrew hers, I didn't have the money for another. So I recycled his. Besides, his seat in the "way back" looked safe enough. In an accident, he'd only fly as far as the middle row. Probably.

Once everyone was strapped in, including me, I started the van and pulled out my vape pen.

"Nana doesn't like you to do that," Colton said, as if delivering a public service announcement.

"Nana's not here," I replied, which was both true and deeply unhelpful.

My mother had pushed me for weeks to contact Joe, and when I finally did, she agreed to watch the kids. Then she got stranded across town because her friend's car died. She shouldn't have even gone out this morning. But try telling my mother anything.

"I'm gonna tell her," Simone warned.

What does it say about me that my children would gleefully snitch on me to their grandmother? I know I should quit. Everyone who vapes knows they should quit. But sometimes you need a hit when life kicks you in the shins, such as when you try to rekindle an old friendship and the guy walks out like you're contagious.

As Colton said, after nine years, he should get over it.

"You hear that, Joe?!" I shouted out the window. "Get over it!" It wasn't the primal scream I'd fantasized about, but it helped.

Colton joined in, yelling, "Yeah, Joe! Get over it!"

I laughed, because honestly, it was perfect.

And I couldn't wait to tell Mom that her grand plan to reunite me with Joe had crashed and burned – exactly as I predicted.

CHAPTER 3

Joe

Friday evening, just as I put my computer into my backpack to leave work, I got a call on my cell phone from the county jail. I should have let it roll to voicemail, but curiosity had me wanting to know what scam *du jour* required impersonating law enforcement.

It was Audrey pleading for bail. Oddly, I wasn't surprised.

Last Sunday, the day after meeting her for coffee, I went to my parents' house – the house I grew up in – to borrow Dad's faucet wrench.

I grew up in the northwest suburbs. Cypress, to be exact. It had plenty of development, but pockets of wildlife remained. As I approached a wooded area that bordered a creek near my old neighborhood, I spotted vultures circling above the road. A pickup truck ahead of me slowed, then swerved around something and kept going. I slowed enough to see a deer lying on the side of the road. In all my years of living in the area, I'd never seen deer in those woods. I'd heard reports of them but never witnessed one firsthand. It was sad that my one encounter was with a dead doe. What did it lack in those woods that it felt the need to cross the street?

A vulture swooped down, then veered off as I passed. The deer moved its head, stretching its neck toward the trees, proving it still had some life left in it. I glanced back to see a fawn standing tiny and alone, watching its mother about to be eaten.

A red traffic light at the intersection gave me time to monitor the scene through the rearview mirror. A minivan stopped next to the deer. The driver, a woman, got out with a phone to her ear and walked around to stand next to the deer. The passenger-side sliding door opened, and a girl of about ten got out, waving her arms to keep the vultures at bay.

A car behind me honked to alert me that the light had turned green.

I'm not usually sensitive to such things. It was an unfortunate accident, certainly, but hunters shoot deer. I've even tagged along with my uncle and cousins to their deer lease north of Austin.

But that night, I dreamed about it. A deer lay on the side of the road, and vultures circled overhead, taking turns swooping down to check the status of their next meal. In the dream, not one but three fawns watched as their mother's life deteriorated. Then the three fawns morphed into Audrey's three kids. They looked up at me as I drove by.

The next morning, I thought I saw Audrey begging at an intersection. I blinked, and it turned out to be a homeless man who bore no resemblance to Audrey. I gave him ten bucks.

Each night, I had an Audrey dream.

In one, she'd fallen into a pit and needed help to get out. In another, men with curled mustaches loaded her into a cage on a horse-drawn wagon. In each dream, her kids watched silently as if they didn't realize the significance of their mother's situation.

I probably shouldn't have told Griffin about it, but at dinner with him yesterday, he sensed something was amiss.

"Dude, you look like crap," he said upon meeting me at Burger Bros.

"I haven't been sleeping well. Not since Saturday. I've been having weird dreams."

"Like what?"

I didn't want to tell him, but I knew he wouldn't let it go unless I gave him something.

"Like, I'm supposed to do something I don't want to do."

Griffin said, "Maybe it's a sign to jump ship. Industry doesn't pay as much, but the hours are better."

I had no problem with the workload at my firm, and besides, giving up multiple clients to serve only one seemed dull. I shrugged and turned the topic to sports.

As we sat across the table from each other, chowing down on burgers, he squinted and appeared to be studying my face. "Your eyes are bloodshot," he noted.

I kept chewing.

"So, sleepless nights," he said. "But it's not a work problem. It can't be a girl problem because you don't have a girlfriend. Finances? You having money problems after buying that house? I told you I'd move in and pay rent after my lease is up."

After he stared at me for several seconds, I caved. "It's Audrey. I mean, her whole situation. Her dad's auto shop went bankrupt a few years ago, and then a couple of years later, he had a heart attack and died. Now she's living with her mom. It's just…. Oh, I don't know."

"So, it's a girl problem after all," Griffin said before taking another bite of his burger. Having a mouth full didn't stop him from asking, "You still have a thing for her, despite boogers and tattoos? Those things mean trauma, probably from sleeping around and having kids with different baby daddies. You don't want to deal with that."

"I definitely don't have a thing for her," I defended.

Griffin threw his hands out, slinging mustard diluted with burger grease onto the table. He swallowed and said, "So what's the issue? She's not your problem. You should get back with Krysta. Cute, smart, and funny."

"You forgot bossy and self-centered," I reminded. Maybe she was the reason I felt a lack of purpose. After realizing she wasn't the one and lamenting the weeks I'd wasted with her, I'd fallen into a slump.

"You're right," he admitted. "Still, she was better than Mindy after she turned into your Bridezilla."

Mindy became so obsessed with planning the perfect wedding that she forgot I was part of it. I may have lost an engagement ring with that one, but that was another bullet I dodged.

That night – last night – my dream had a Star Wars theme. A hologram projection of a princess said, "Help me, Obi-Wan Kenobi. You're my only hope." Except that the princess was Audrey.

But those dreams and the conversation with Griffin had just been academic until Audrey's call from jail. I stared at my phone for several seconds after the call ended. I learned that she'd been there since Wednesday, her mother was on a cruise with a gentleman friend, and her brother refused to help. I'd just committed to bailing her out for stealing a car.

* * *

Audrey looked better upon release from jail than she did a week ago at the coffee shop. Her black running shorts and faded red T-shirt may not have been as fashionable, but the jailors had made her remove her piercings, which got my stamp of approval. Other than the little indentations in her cheeks where the dimple thorns had been, her face looked more like the version I knew in high school. Her outfit also let me confirm she had more tattoos than I'd seen last week. At least one more: an image of a sleeping baby on her right thigh. Like her left arm, her left leg had no tattoos.

As we left the jailhouse, she clutched my arm during the two-block walk to the car as if someone might grab her and drag her back. Or grab her bag of jewelry. I was more concerned with being assaulted by people leaving the facility, or even those picking up people leaving the facility. Unkempt hair, men with neckbeards, plenty of tattoos. I know it was an unreasonable concern, what with police and deputies going in and out. I had to check my bias against tattooed people since I now escorted one to my car. Or maybe picking her up from jail should confirm it.

The walk to the parking lot was punctuated by a string of "thank you," "I'm sorry," "I owe you big time," and "I'll borrow money from my mom to pay you back."

After I started the car, I asked, "Stealing a car? Really?"

"It's just a misunderstanding," she defended.

As much as I wanted to know the story, I also wanted to leave the area as soon as possible. "Where am I taking you? Your parents' place?" I still hadn't adjusted to the fact that her father had passed away, and she now had only one parent.

"Liam's house. He's got the kids." Then, as if remembering that I didn't know where her brother lived, she added, "Katy. He lives in Katy. Just start driving, and I'll tell you where to go."

I let out a sigh and shook my head slightly. "Your brother can take care of your kids, but won't bail you out?"

She ignored my question and said, "I should let him know we're coming."

I pulled out of the parking lot and drove toward the freeway.

Audrey picked up the loose end of my phone charging cable, examined the plug, and then issued an "Ugh."

"What?"

"My phone's dead, and your cable's not compatible."

I picked up my phone from a cupholder and tapped the screen to wake it up. I held it up to my face just long enough to unlock it and passed it to Audrey.

After a brief call to Liam, she put the phone on the center console, tilted her head back, and closed her eyes. "He hates me. It's a long story."

I waited until we entered the freeway to ask about the charges that landed her in jail.

"I stopped making payments on the van," she said. "I lost my babysitter, then lost my job, and ran out of money."

That didn't make sense. "I didn't think they arrested people for that," I said. "I thought they just repossessed the vehicle."

"This wasn't through a company. I was renting it from a guy I knew in Beaumont. Then I moved back home and forgot to make payments."

"A guy, huh? One of your boyfriends?"

"One of?" she asked indignantly. "You think I have loads of them?"

I quickly reviewed the limited conversation at the coffee shop last week. Three kids, each with a different dad. She mentioned the first dad was one of the guys she met in Europe. *One of.* Yes, I thought she had loads of boyfriends over the years. After paying $800 to a bail bondsman to get her out of jail, I should be allowed to make a few reasonable judgments about her personal life. Nevertheless, her question was probably best left unanswered.

I muttered, "Sorry," although I really wasn't.

She grabbed my phone again and held it up to my face. I moved my head to see around it, and she moved the phone again.

"What are you doing?"

She pulled the phone away and said, "Trying to unlock your phone again."

Apparently, it worked, as she then opened the browser and tapped out a quick search. A few seconds later, the sound of dialing came through the car's speakers. Upon making the connection, I heard a masculine voice answer, "Art-Bow Towing. Leave a message after the tone."

Audrey didn't waste time with polite greetings. "Dimitri! It's Audrey. I can't believe you had me arrested! Call me back at this number." She ended the call and muttered something that sounded like Copenhagen.

CHAPTER 4

Audrey

My kids – and approximately half the neighborhood – got front-row seats to me being handcuffed and stuffed into the back of a patrol car like I'd been caught running a meth lab. I'm sure it was the most exciting thing to happen on our street since the Great HOA Potluck of 2019. That's my role in this suburb: providing free entertainment and cautionary tales.

I yelled at my kids to go to Ms. Stacy's house next door. I didn't actually *ask* Stacy, but she saw the whole circus, heard me shout the instructions, and didn't object. In my book, silence equals consent – and free childcare. That's where my sister-in-law eventually found them, after I called my brother and begged him to pick them up.

Joe was not exactly at the top of my "people to call when arrested" list. Nothing like a crisis to remind you how tiny your support network really is. I called Mom first, but she was off on a cruise out of Miami with her dentist boyfriend, probably sipping margaritas and pretending she didn't have adult children. I left a message. Then I called my brother. Left another message. Then I waited. Two hours. Nothing.

I forgave Mom – she was probably somewhere in the Bermuda Triangle with zero bars of service. But Liam? Oh, he got the message. His wife, Cami, probably told him to let me marinate in jail a little. She thinks I'm a "bad influence" on her precious Hannah, which is hilarious because Hannah once bit a kid at preschool for touching her glitter glue. I could practically hear the argument they had before Cami drove over to retrieve my kids from the neighbor's house.

Three days. I spent three full *Finland* days in jail. On day two, someone asked if I had a lawyer. I didn't, so they assigned me one. On day three, I finally stood before a judge.

After reading my charges, he asked, "How do you plead?"

My court-appointed lawyer whispered that I shouldn't plead guilty, so I said, "Not guilty." Not because I didn't take the van – I absolutely did – but because apparently the only way to explain yourself to a judge is to pretend you didn't do the thing you definitely did.

Then the judge set bail. Cue another round of calls to Mom and Liam. Mom didn't answer. Liam refused. And that's when I remembered the coffee shop. Fortunately, my lawyer convinced the jail staff to let me dig Joe's number out of my phone before the battery died its dramatic, gasping death.

Last week, Joe's face did this weird thing when he saw me. First, a smile – small, polite, hopeful. Then, when he realized the tattooed disaster in front of him was actually me, the smile evaporated like it had somewhere better to be. He tried to recover, but I saw the disappointment. Maybe I overshared. Maybe I overshared *a lot*. His eyes kept darting toward the door like he was planning an escape route. I tried to get him talking about himself, but apparently he'd reached his limit and made an excuse to leave.

Thinking about that while standing at the jail phone made me want to cry. Like I was at the bottom of a deep, echoing well, shouting for help while everyone else was busy living normal, non-felony-adjacent lives.

When I called Joe, I didn't expect anything. Not a thing.

But then he answered. And he came.

* * *

We'd just picked up the kids from Liam's house, where I got the obligatory scolding from Cami, slightly more intense than usual, and were on the way home when Dimitri called. Unfortunately for me, the call came through the car speakers again.

"Hello, Audrey."

I got straight to the point. "The police came to my mom's house and arrested me for stealing the van!" They were actually sheriff's deputies, but it's easier to say police.

"My van that you ran off with!" he shouted back. "Maybe if you'd answered my calls, we could have avoided this."

Joe thought he could join the conversation. "Why didn't you just come take the van? Why go to the police?"

"Who are you?" Dimitri demanded. "New boyfriend? Good luck. Just know she don't pay her bills."

I give a zip-it gesture across my lips to indicate to Joe to stay out of it.

"He's a friend," I told Dimitri.

"Well, Mr. Friend, I would have, if I knew where she ran off to. I couldn't find her, and she wouldn't call me. I had no choice but to report it stolen."

"And give them my name," I complained.

"Of course. We had a deal, Audrey. Weekly payments. You could pay in cash, or you could pay in pus-…"

"Dimitri!" I shouted to drown out his words. "My kids are here."

He grunted and said, "We're done." The phone went dead.

We only had about two seconds of peace before Royce piped up with, "Momma."

I twisted around to see him wedged between his siblings in the back seat like a human sandwich filling. Joe's car wasn't built for three child seats across – honestly, only minivans and SUVs can handle that level of parental Tetris. "Yes, Honey?"

"How did you pay for the van with a cat?"

I blinked. "What?"

"Mr. Dimitri said you could pay with cash or with a kitty cat."

Kitty was… not the word Dimitri used. Clearly my attempt to drown out his voice had failed.

Joe shot me a sideways glance and grunted, the universal male sound for *I'm not getting involved, but I'm absolutely judging you.*

"Well…," I began, scrambling for a kid-friendly explanation. "Mr. Dimitri really likes cats, but he's not allowed to have one where he lives. So, I told him we had a cat."

"We didn't have a cat," Royce said, ever the fact-checker.

"Remember that stray cat that used to hang around our apartment? I told Dimitri it was ours."

Joe jumped in, oh-so-helpfully. "So, you let Dimitri play with your kitty if he would let you use his van."

I shot him the universal *zip it* gesture. He turned back to the road before he could see my face contort into a full-body grimace.

"Sometimes I was still awake when he came over," Royce added.

Now *that* grimace was for a whole different reason. "It was past your bedtime, and we tried to be quiet."

"Is that why you went to your bedroom?"

"Yeah, baby. We didn't want to wake you up."

And that, I decided, was the end of this conversation before someone asked for more details and I had to fling myself out of the moving vehicle.

CHAPTER 5

Joe

Audrey's house hadn't changed much since I'd last seen it nine years ago. The most notable difference was the For Sale sign in the yard.

But that's not where we ended up. Audrey didn't have her house key; Royce had given it to the neighbor, Stacy. The kids and I waited in the car in the driveway while she went to Stacy's house for the key.

Two minutes later, she returned to the car.

"No one's home."

She borrowed my phone again.

With her brother on the line, she asked, "Did Stacy give Cami our house key when she picked up the kids?"

After listening to a reply, she grumbled, "Well, that's just great," and ended the call without saying goodbye.

With her eyes squeezed shut, she said, "I don't know if I should break a window, or what."

Her tightly closed eyes didn't stop the tears from streaming down her cheeks.

I brought them home. My home. The home with no accommodation for overnight guests. At least not until we stopped at Target to buy air mattresses, pillows, and blankets. Audrey also insisted on toothbrushes and toothpaste.

I led them through the back door, past the small four-chair dinette in the breakfast nook, which adjoined the galley-style kitchen, and then onward through the living room, flipping on lights along the way. The living room had only a sofa and a coffee table, leaving plenty of space for more furniture. I ushered them to continue to the hallway to the bedrooms, but they couldn't help but slow down and look around, including straying from the path to look into the formal dining room off the front entry hall. The dining room had no dining table. The rooms were devoid of art.

"Why is it so empty?" Royce asked.

Audrey looked at me, waiting for an answer.

"I only brought the furniture I had at my old apartment. I planned on renting out the bedrooms to a couple of friends and figured they would bring more furniture to fill up the place."

Audrey nodded her acceptance of my explanation. "I guess everyone's got to start somewhere."

"We didn't bring any furniture with us when we left our old place," Royce said. "Good thing Nana already had furniture."

"It was just thrift store junk, anyway," Audrey explained.

"As you can see," I said. "I haven't done much with the place. The cabinets and fixtures are dated, but everything works. 'Well-maintained' is how the real estate agent described it. I'm not a big fan of the gray walls. I want to paint everything, but haven't gotten around to it. The only thing new is the flooring. It was a mishmash of carpet, ceramic tile, and laminate." I tapped my foot on the floor and said, "My dad and I put this in."

"Real wood?" Audrey asked.

She probably wouldn't have asked if she saw it in the daylight.

"Vinyl plank," I confessed.

"Nice," she said.

I couldn't tell if she was sincere or just polite. I accepted her approval, regardless. Even if she were just being polite, I was proud of my and Dad's effort, and the floor looks a hundred times better than it did when I moved in.

"Let me show you the bedrooms."

I led the group to the bedroom at the front of the house and set the air pump and one of the two queen size air beds on the floor. "This will be the boy room," I said.

I looked at the boys, each of whom carried a newly purchased pillow. "You can put those down. Royce, do you know how to blow up an air mattress?"

"No," he said, setting his pillow on the floor gently as if it were breakable.

Colton held his over his head and threw it across the room, hitting the wall before falling to the floor.

"I'll show you later," I said. "Then you can help your mom inflate the other bed."

I took the shopping bag from Audrey, pulled out a neatly packaged blanket, and dropped it onto the floor next to the box with the air mattress. Then I walked past them to the hallway and led them to the middle bedroom.

"This will be the girl room."

My golf bag stood in the middle of the room as if on display. I set the shopping bag and the other air mattress next to the golf bag, then dragged the bag to the closet. Simone walked to the middle of the room and extended her arm to allow her pillow to drop onto the floor next to the shopping bag with the remaining pillow and blanket. With her small stature, the pillow didn't have far to fall.

"Joe," Audrey said. "I know you didn't have to do any of this. I'll make it up to you. I promise."

I didn't know how she could do that. She'd mentioned working part-time as a waitress in the evenings while her mom watched the kids, but I imagined the income would barely cover groceries and her phone bill, let alone repay the bail.

CHAPTER 6

Audrey

After getting the kids scrubbed, rinsed, and tucked in like slightly feral burritos, I headed to the master bedroom to find Joe. I opened the door and heard the shower running in his bathroom – the one part of the house that had apparently escaped from 1974. According to Joe, the previous owners were an older couple who heroically replaced the avocado-green tub with a walk-in shower complete with a glass door and a built-in tile bench. Luxury, if you ignored everything else.

I slipped back out and took a tour of the house, which lasted a grand total of five minutes. There was a wet bar with a sink that didn't work, a fireplace with no screen, and furniture that looked like it had been collected from three different garage sales and one curbside giveaway. Joe wasn't flashy, sure, but I expected at least one matching set of something.

I found a pen on the coffee table and immediately stuck it in my mouth. For the past three days, I'd been desperate to have *something* between my lips – a cigarette, a vape, a straw, a stick of licorice, literally anything. The mechanics at Dad's shop had introduced me to cigarettes, and I switched to vaping when I got pregnant with Colton. Tonight, the pen would have to serve as my emotional support nicotine substitute.

In the kitchen, I started flipping light switches. One of them turned on the garbage disposal, which I shut off so fast I nearly sprained a finger. No way was I waking those kids. Across from the entrance to the table-free dining room, a pair of folding doors hid the washer and dryer. Next to the dining entrance was a pantry roughly the size of a shoebox. Apparently, people in the 1970s survived on canned soup and hope.

I tiptoed back to Simone's room, grabbed my pillow, and carried it to Joe's room. The shower was off now. I tapped on the door with my fingernail, removed the pen from my mouth like I was about to deliver a speech, and walked in.

The sink area was open to the bedroom, so I immediately spotted Joe standing there in shorts and a T-shirt, flossing like he was preparing for a dental Olympics. He didn't notice me until I reached the end of the bed.

He glanced up. "You need something?"

I tossed my pillow onto the head of the bed next to his and sat down. "You've done so much for me – for us – today. I know it'll take a while before I can pay you back." I leaned back on my elbows, lowered my voice, and added, "But I want to show my appreciation tonight."

CHAPTER 7

Joe

I couldn't believe her! She came to my bedroom, lay back on my bed in front of me, and then spread her legs. At least she wore shorts. I couldn't help but glance from her face with its booger ring to her open legs, then back to the booger ring. Her audacity both amazed and disgusted me. I hadn't seen her in so long, she was practically a stranger. Yet after only a few hours together, she was ready to jump into bed with me. It's no wonder she has three kids with different men; I don't think she understood how babies are made. Besides, the septum ring made her offer even less tempting.

While we dated all those years ago, we'd never had sex. Sure, we had a few awesome make-out sessions, but we never went all the way. I thought it was by mutual consent. If you do that with someone whom you're not ready to commit your life to, what do you have left to give your soul mate? I wouldn't serve leftovers to royalty. Strangely, I think her dad would have beaten the crap out of me, while respecting me more at the same time. His values were messed up, but that's a different story.

"We're not doing that," I told her.

Her smile evaporated, and she quickly closed her legs. "Oh, I just thought…." She stood up and, in a barely audible voice, muttered, "I'm such an idiot." In her normal voice, she said, "You're probably tired. I am, too. We should just get some sleep."

With that statement, I expected her to leave. Instead, she moved to the side of the bed, pulled back the covers, and climbed in.

"No, no, no," I said. "You need to go sleep with Simone."

With her forehead wrinkled and her mouth open, she looked as if I'd just spoken a foreign language. When she closed her mouth into a frown, I couldn't tell if she was about to cry or chew me out. Fortunately, she did neither. She merely slid out of bed, picked up her pillow, and left.

* * *

I dreamed about her again. I pretty much expected the dreams nowadays.

A chain ran from a metal ring around Audrey's neck to a steel bar attached to the back wall of the auction platform. She stared at an empty spot on the floor between the platform and my place in the back. Chains dangling from the bar served as reminders of slaves already sold. Audrey was the last to be offered, and the bidding started low.

The bidders appeared to be the dregs of society. A skinny man with so many tattoos, he looked like a lizard with poor teeth. A short, middle-aged man with a bad combover and a lustful sneer. A six-foot-six, three-hundred-and-fifty-pound mountain of a man who often licked his lips and had a ribbon of condom packets hanging from a back pocket.

Three small figures appeared in a back row I hadn't noticed earlier. As the bidding started, all three turned and looked at me. Royce, Colton, and Simone. They showed no look of sadness or horror or any emotions at all. They seemed to merely acknowledge my presence at an event they'd seen before.

I woke up before the bidding ended, hating myself for this strange obsession with Audrey.

CHAPTER 8

Audrey

My father used to ask me after every date with Joe if he'd "tried to get in my pants." As if I'd ever report that to him like some kind of romantic progress update. For the record, Joe never did. My brother, ever the supportive sibling, used to tease that Joe was gay and using me as cover. I never saw any evidence of that – unless enthusiastic kissing is now considered a symptom – but after last night, I briefly wondered if I needed to reevaluate my entire romantic résumé. I don't put myself out there for just anyone. And the ones I *did* put myself out for never turned me down. Until Joe.

I don't know when I finally fell asleep. I'd barely slept the last two nights, and Simone kept shifting around like a tiny, restless octopus. But at some point, exhaustion must've tackled me, because when I woke up, sunlight was blasting through the blinds like it had something to prove – and Simone was gone.

I was already halfway upright when she shrieked, "Mommy! Mommy!"

I followed the sound to the living room, where she was bouncing on her toes by the sliding glass door like a caffeinated meerkat. "Mr. Joe has a playground!"

He did indeed. Out back stood a playset with two swings, a little tower, a climbing wall, a slide, and a canopy that looked like it had survived a mild tornado. Colton and Royce were already on the tower, waving like they were on a parade float. Colton slid down the slide and sprinted toward us, yelling for Simone to join them.

"Go on, Honey," I said, opening the door. Then I went looking for Joe.

After searching the house, I checked the garage. His car was gone. Eventually, I found a sticky note on the bathroom mirror: *I'll be back in a few hours. – Joe.*

My first thought: he was avoiding us. Then I corrected myself: he was avoiding *me.* That look he gave me last night had pierced me deeper than any of my piercings. No one ever did something for me without expecting something in return. Especially not men. And they all expected the same thing. Except Joe. With other men, I'd sometimes felt dirty, sometimes defeated. I did what I had to do to keep my kids fed and sheltered. But this time? I just felt embarrassed. Ashamed.

Royce snapped me out of my pity spiral with a very practical, "I'm hungry."

I checked the fridge and pantry. The fridge held beer, milk, eggs, jelly, and ham lunchmeat. The pantry offered Honey Bunches of Oats, bread, and peanut butter.

"Typical bachelor," I muttered. A man could survive a nuclear winter with this setup, but heaven forbid he own a vegetable.

The real challenge? Joe had exactly two plates and two bowls, but enough plastic cups from Burger Bros to host a children's birthday party. I made scrambled eggs and supplemented them with cereal. We took turns using the dishes like pioneers, if pioneers had access to refrigerators and questionable bachelor pantries.

CHAPTER 9

Joe

Dimitri didn't fit the description of any of the men in my dream. He appeared to be in his mid-forties, with neatly trimmed salt-and-pepper hair and muscular arms covered in tattoos that went from the backs of his hands, up his arms, and disappeared under the sleeves of his tight Art-Bow Towing shirt. I wondered if he represented Audrey's type. He probably fit her father's view of what her type should be.

As we waited outside the bank for it to open, I got the feeling he was trying to size me up. I had no doubt he would win in a fight. I dressed in faded jeans, a plain blue T-shirt, and worn sneakers. I tried to look like someone of meager means in case he thought of upping the amount we'd discussed on the phone.

"Welcome to Beaumont," he said after I introduced myself.

I took a chance to call him early, hoping he didn't like to sleep in on Saturdays. Apparently, he didn't.

Before giving me a chance to respond, he asked, "So, what's the story with you and Audrey? Are you lovers?"

Was he jealous? A jilted boyfriend? "No," I assured. "We're just friends. We go way back."

He looked like he didn't buy that story. "Why are you willing to pay what she owed?"

I took a deep breath. The truth is, I didn't know the answer. It just felt like something I needed to do. "I don't want to see her go to jail. I mean, she's got three kids who need her."

"I wouldn't trust that cunt, if I were you. She may sound all sweet and innocent when she wants something, but in the end, she won't appreciate what you've done for her."

That's what I was afraid of. I had plenty of time during the hour-and-a-half drive to berate myself for putting up treasure for what might be a lost cause. I hadn't even settled on what the cause was. Was Audrey worth it? I'd forgotten about her until a week ago. Now she haunts my dreams.

"After I pay you," I said, "you'll sign a statement that she's all paid up and doesn't owe you anything else, right?"

"Sure, I'll sign whatever you want as long as I get the money."

I had the statement prepared on my laptop, which I carried in my backpack. "Good. I'll get the bank to print it out for us. Two copies, one for each of us. Then they can notarize it."

He grunted and said, "You've thought of everything."

He'd asked about my relationship with Audrey, so I thought it fair to ask him the same. "Were you and she, uh, dating?"

He chuckled, tilted his head slightly as if my question amused him, and then held up his left hand and wiggled the finger with a wedding band. "It was strictly business. I had something she needed, and she had something I needed." He seemed to confuse needs with wants.

The bank manager unlocked the door and motioned for us to come in.

When our transaction was done, complete with Dimitri's signed and notarized statement, he said, "I appreciate your three thousand bucks, but I think you're a sucker. She's a taker, not a giver."

I winced at the dollar amount. A hundred dollars per missed week, plus interest. I tried to negotiate it down, but he threw in a late payment fee to raise it to an even three thousand.

"But you'll drop the charges, right?"

He tucked the cashier's check into his pocket and snickered. "That's not up to me. Only the DA can drop the charges."

A knot formed in my stomach, and I groaned inwardly. Yeah, I'm a sucker. To both Audrey and Dimitri. He has no control over the charges and scammed me out of three thousand dollars. I felt my temperature rising. "So, you get your van back, and you get my money, and we get nothing in return?"

"The insurance company paid for the van months ago. It ain't mine anymore." He tapped the pocket with the check. "This is icing on the cake."

Then he patted my cheek and said, "I'll call the DA's office and tell them y'all made good on the debt. Maybe they'll reduce her sentence."

He turned and walked toward his tow truck, leaving me searching for a way to salvage the situation. I remembered his wedding ring and the "strictly business" comment.

"You know," I called after him, "I think you'd prefer this doesn't go to court."

He turned and called back, "Why is that?"

"They might not like your alternative payment plan. Sex for hire could get you in trouble."

He smirked and waved his hand as if dismissing me. "Call a lawyer."

I'm such an idiot.

CHAPTER 10

Audrey

Joe arrived in a mood so sour it could've curdled milk. I'd expected at least a chuckle when he saw us – because honestly, the kids and I had already laughed ourselves silly over our new fashion choices.

"You went through my things," he said in an accusatory tone.

I did *not* confess that I'd looked through every drawer, closet, and suspiciously lumpy storage bin in the house. I didn't find any skeletons – literal or metaphorical – but I couldn't deny the obvious.

"The kids got dirty outside, and I had to wash their clothes. Besides, I've been wearing the same outfit since yesterday." Which was true. I'd arrived with nothing but the clothes I'd worn to jail four days ago. Not exactly a capsule wardrobe.

The kids, meanwhile, each wore one of Joe's shirts as a dress or tunic. No pants. No underwear. Just a shirt. Thankfully, they were small enough that everything important stayed covered. The boys wore golf shirts. Simone wore a white undershirt like an oversized sundress.

Colton lifted his shirt and proudly announced, "Look! I'm not wearing underpants!"

"I am, though," I assured Joe, dissolving into giggles. His green plaid boxers peeked out from under the blue button-down I'd stolen from his closet. I still don't understand how men cram that much fabric into jeans. Doesn't it bunch? Doesn't it chafe? But hey – boxers look better on men than briefs. And, frankly, they looked fantastic on me.

Joe groaned and shook his head like he was reconsidering every life choice that had led him to this moment.

"Our clothes should be ready soon," I said. "I put them in the dryer about fifteen minutes ago. I did your laundry, too." Then, casually, "Where did you go?"

I'd meant to call him while he was out, but between wrangling the kids and updating Mom on my recent adventures in incarceration, I got distracted. Joe pulled a sheet of paper from his backpack and slapped it on the table like he was presenting Exhibit A.

"What's that?"

"Evidence that I paid off Dimitri."

I picked up the paper. Saw the amount. Saw Dimitri's signature. My brain short-circuited. I hadn't meant to drag Joe this deep into my mess.

"You went to see Dimitri?"

He nodded.

"And you paid what I owed him?"

"Yep. I just gave three thousand dollars to a sexual predator for possibly no benefit."

I wasn't sure my arrangement with Dimitri technically qualified him for that title, but I wasn't about to argue semantics. "Why is there no benefit?"

"Because he can't drop the charges."

"Only the DA can do that," I said.

"Apparently, everybody knows that but me."

Royce shrugged. "I didn't know."

I smiled. Joe did not.

"Thanks, buddy," Joe muttered, trudging to the sofa. He plopped down, crossed his arms, and stared at the floor under the TV, which was currently playing *Perry Winkle, Kid Sleuth*. I don't think he even noticed Simone sitting at the other end, quietly eating imaginary popcorn.

I grabbed a beer from the fridge, sat beside him, popped the top, and placed it in his hand. "You're a good man. No one else would do what you did. My brother wouldn't. I didn't mean to drag you into this."

He kept staring at the floor. "I tried to help," he said. "But I don't think it did any good."

"Bailing me out was good, wasn't it?" I said.

He didn't answer. He looked like he was weighing whether leaving me in jail might've been the more peaceful option. Maybe I was a lost cause. But I'd pay him back somehow. Eventually. Probably.

The dryer buzzed, announcing that at least *one* thing in this house was ready to move forward.

* * *

It took a while to get Joe out of his funk. I made him a grilled ham and cheese sandwich and dragged him to the kitchen table to eat it. Simone and Colton peppered him with questions while I folded our clothes at the coffee table.

Colton asked, "Why do you have a playground if you don't have kids?"

"It came with the house," Joe explained. "I thought about putting it up for sale, but never got around to it."

Simone called out, "Mommy, can we buy it?"

"Honey, where would we put it? Remember, Nana's selling her house."

Colton, again: "Mommy found a soccer ball in the closet. Do you play soccer?"

Nothing like having my own kid rat me out for snooping. I glanced over at Joe to see his reaction. He paused his chewing, locked eyes with me, and raised his eyebrows. I just smiled and continued folding the clothes, not acknowledging my sin.

He looked back at Colton and said, "I used to play, but it's been a while."

"Me and Royce played soccer today," Colton said.

"It wasn't real playing," Royce corrected. "Just kicking the ball with the kids across the street."

Imagine pro players having to dodge trees and flowerbeds on their way to score. Maybe that would get more Americans to watch.

"This street?" Joe asked, as if surprised that kids lived on his street.

"Yeah," Colton answered. "They were nice. Then the sprinklers came on, and everyone got wet."

That was my cue. "Come on, kids. Let's put our own clothes back on so Joe can take us home."

CHAPTER 11

Joe

I still felt like a fool for paying Audrey's sleazy friend without checking out how the criminal justice process works. Audrey said it would probably help her case. I hoped so, for her kids' sake. She also said she would pay me back, but I didn't expect to ever see that money again. She had to pause her waitress job while her babysitter – her mother – went on vacation. And she could end up back in jail in a few weeks.

I should have expected her to look around. What else would she do while stuck in a strange house with three kids? Her exploration must have paid off because she found my old charging cord that was compatible with her phone. She contacted her mother, just off the cruise ship in Miami, and then reached out to her neighbor about the house key.

I drove them home after lunch. That is, after Audrey put away my laundry, cleaned up the kitchen, and had her kids change back into their regular clothes. I suppose going commando and without pants in oversized shirts was against even her questionable standards. The clean-up was at her insistence, not mine.

* * *

On Sunday morning, I found Dimitri's affidavit of receiving payment still on the kitchen table. I texted Audrey to tell her I'd bring it over.

An hour later, she responded, "We'll come get it. Mom will be home soon, and she wants to see your house."

In the early afternoon, Audrey's mother stood at my front door with Audrey and the kids.

As soon as I opened the door, she pushed her way past the kids and pulled me in for a hug. "Joe! It's so good to see you! After that mess with Audrey after high school, I didn't think we'd ever see you again."

Did she mean the breakup or Audrey getting pregnant in Europe? "Hi, Mrs. Harris."

"You're an adult now, so call me Beverly. Nice neighborhood. Reminds me of the one I grew up in."

The years must have been more kind to her than they were to Audrey. Mrs. Harris was about the same age as my mother but looked years younger.

I moved aside and motioned for them to enter. "Come in."

Not knowing what else to say and feeling awkward, I said, "I'm sorry about Mr. Harris."

I wasn't really. Audrey claimed her dad's insults were mere jokes, not to be taken seriously. But to teenage me, they went beyond friendly banter. According to him, I drove the wrong car, did the wrong sport, and had the wrong career goals. He twisted everything about me into a dig against my manhood. I wasn't like the real men he and Audrey's brother were, working dirty jobs and having played football in high school.

"Thank you," Mrs. Harris – Beverly – responded.

Searching for a safe topic, I said, "I noticed the 'For Sale' sign at your house."

"The property taxes are killing me," she said. "We didn't have much besides the house after the business went belly up. I want to buy a tiny house and park it at my brother's place. He's got ten acres near Brookshire. I'll save the rest of the money from the sale for retirement."

"Sounds fiscally responsible," I agreed.

"Yeah, but Audrey threw a wrench in the gears when she moved back last fall. But enough of my problems. Show me your house."

The kids took that as their cue to take over.

"Nana, come look at our rooms," Colton said, already heading to the hallway.

The way he said it sounded cute and disturbing at the same time. He didn't describe them as where they had stayed, but "our" rooms, a possessive pronoun.

The rest of us followed. He rushed into the bedroom he'd shared with Royce and fell onto the air mattress that I hadn't bothered to put away. "This is my room," he proudly proclaimed.

"Mine, too," Royce said.

"I see," Beverly said as she walked in to stand next to the mattress. "Is that a queen or full?" A strangely irrelevant question.

"Queen," I said.

"This is a good-sized room for kids," Beverly said. "Are you planning for the future, Joe?"

"Just building equity," I told her. "I'm planning on renting out the extra rooms."

Simone grabbed her grandmother's hand and pulled her toward the doorway. "I slept with Mommy in there," she said, pointing to the middle bedroom.

"How did you like staying with Uncle Liam and Aunt Cami?" Beverly asked.

"Aunt Cami's always grumpy," Royce said.

"And Mommy wasn't there," Simone added. She lowered her voice to a whisper and said, "The police took her to jail."

* * *

After the house tour, the kids pulled Audrey outside to climb on the playset; them, not Audrey. Her mom held me back, and we watched from inside the living room.

She placed her hand on my arm and said, "You know, it wasn't Audrey's idea to break up with you. Her dad pushed her to it."

"I never understood what he had against me."

"It wasn't really you," she said, basically admitting that Mr. Harris did have something against me. "It was your parents."

"My parents? I don't remember him ever meeting my parents."

"You drove that little Volkswagen with a funny bumper sticker on the back. Something about the president."

"Yeah," I acknowledged. Audrey's dad said my Golf GTI was a woman's car. The sticker was left over from the previous owner and didn't specifically refer to the president. It said, Don't blame me, I didn't vote for him.

Mrs. Harris – Beverly – continued, "Your mom brought it to our shop for repair, and then she wasn't happy with the cost when it was done. Your dad accused Bill of doing unnecessary work and jacking up the price. They had a pretty heated discussion. A few months later, you showed up in our driveway in that car."

Based on her explanation, Mr. Harris didn't like me because of something my parents did. But the story didn't add up. "My dad always took our cars to a shop near Jersey Village," I told her. "He's known the head mechanic there for years."

"Well, I don't know about that, but Bill was convinced he knew your Volkswagen." She paused before assuring, "But I've always liked you."

I shrugged. With a dad like Mr. Harris, maybe breaking up was for the best. Then I remembered we bought the car from someone in the neighborhood the summer before eleventh grade. Mr. Harris hated me for a grudge against a neighbor I barely knew.

Beverly went on, "The day after prom, her dad badgered her again about you. That's when she brought up the Europe trip. Her cousin was going backpacking through Europe and invited her along."

"Lainey." I'm surprised I remembered her cousin's name. Lainey graduated from college when Audrey graduated from high school. I didn't know she'd invited Audrey to go with her.

"I was opposed. Bill, too," she said. "Audrey was too young to be flitting around Europe, and I didn't think she was interested in it. But then Bill pressed her about breaking up again."

We paused in awkward silence. After a moment, she continued, "So Audrey told him she would leave you if he paid for Europe."

I'd been looking at Mrs. Harris as she talked, but I turned to the window to watch Audrey pushing her youngest on the swing. "So, she traded me for a European vacation."

"Joe, she was bluffing, and her dad called her bluff. They were both stubborn. What's that dangerous game where people drive their cars toward each other, waiting for the other to swerve away at the last second?"

"Chicken."

"And you know what happens if no one swerves."

I looked at Mrs. Harris again. "Three kids, a neck tattoo, and a face full of metal?"

I didn't realize her hand was still on my arm until she squeezed it. "That came later. After her dad kicked her out, we didn't see her for a couple of years. She showed up at the funeral looking like that." Beverly removed her hand to wave it across her face. "And with two more kids than she left with."

She turned to look outside again. "Joe, you're a good man for helping her."

The compliment should have been welcomed; however, my stomach knotted at the reminder. I felt that some divine force had compelled me to help. I'm supposed to feel good about it, right?

Then I asked about a topic I should have left alone. "What will Audrey do when you sell the house?"

"I don't know. I can't afford to take care of her. She'll probably have to go on welfare again. At least that's better than shacking up with some sugar daddy."

Again? She had been on welfare before? It was hard to believe that one of my friends, someone who grew up solidly in the middle class, maybe even considered upper middle class, could have been on welfare. Did I live in a bubble? I looked back at the coffee table where yesterday Audrey had folded my clothes, then at the kitchen table, where she'd served me a grilled sandwich. Then I looked outside, past the swing set to the sky above it, focusing on a distant cloud, and whispered, "Why me?"

"Pardon?" her mother asked.

Years ago, I stood at the edge of a cliff over a river, preparing to jump. All the bravado I had before stepping to the edge evaporated. Had my friends not been watching, I might have turned around. But I squeezed my eyes shut, took a deep breath, and launched myself into the void.

I opened the sliding glass door and called out, "Can y'all come in? I have a proposal."

I swear the sun blinked at me.

CHAPTER 12

Audrey

When Joe said, "I have a proposal," Royce immediately blurted, "You want to marry my mom?"

Honestly, sometimes my kids leap to conclusions so wild they should come with a safety harness. But he was only eight, so I tried not to laugh directly in his face. Thankfully, Joe saved Royce's dignity before I snorted.

"Not that kind of proposal," Joe said, looking mildly horrified.

He motioned for us to sit on the sofa while he dragged a kitchen chair over like he was about to conduct a very serious job interview. Simone perched on my mom's lap, and the rest of us stared at him as if he was about to announce the winners of a raffle.

Joe stammered like a kid who forgot his lines in the school play. "I…um…my house…uh…."

He cleared his throat and tried again, this time locking eyes with me like he was bracing for impact. "Your mom is selling her house. You and your kids need a place to stay. And I have the extra bedrooms."

Men have asked me to move in before, but usually after at least a few dates and a questionable life choice or two. "Are you asking us to move in?"

His Adam's apple bobbed like it was trying to escape. "Yeah. I'm offering you a place to stay."

He didn't look thrilled about it. Then again, the last two days had been…a lot. Didn't he call me a lost cause? Or maybe I called myself that. Hard to keep track.

"Me *and* the kids, right?"

He blinked at me as if I'd asked whether gravity still worked. Even Mom looked confused.

She answered for him. "Of course he's including the kids, Audrey."

"I won't be able to pay anything," I warned. "I only work part-time. And that's only because Mom watches the kids at night."

"I don't expect you to pay anything," Joe said. "I'd expect you to keep the place clean, cook for me—for us—and do my laundry. And whatever else makes life easier."

Given his bachelor lifestyle, "housekeeping" probably meant picking up socks and occasionally wiping a counter.

Colton sat beside me, and Royce watched from the fireplace hearth like a tiny judge presiding over the proceedings. I noticed him glance toward the front door. Outside, the neighbor kids were shrieking with joy. He clearly wanted to join them.

"Royce, you can go if you want."

"I want to hear this first," he said, as if this were a congressional hearing.

I turned back to Joe. "Okay. But I need a guarantee."

Mom gasped like I'd just demanded a blood oath. She seemed more offended than Joe.

Joe stood abruptly. "Just a minute. I need a notepad."

He disappeared down the hall and returned with a notepad and pen, scooting his chair closer like he was about to draft a legally binding treaty. He wrote at the top: *JOE: Room and Board – Est. $24,000.*

A few lines down, he wrote: *AUDREY.*

Then he listed:

- *Clean house: dust, vacuum, toilets, etc.*
- *Laundry*
- *Cook*

At least he didn't assign dollar amounts. My parents used to pay a housekeeper weekly, and even *she* didn't make what Joe could charge for rent.

Mom chimed in, "She can also make your lunches for work."

"Mom, it's his list," I protested. Whose side was she on?

"What? I did that for your father all the time."

Joe added *Lunch and Dinner* under Cook, then looked up at me. "What did you want to add?"

"School starts in a few weeks. If we do this, you have to commit to letting us stay the whole school year."

"That's a good point," Mom said. "You can't kick them out in the middle of the school year."

Joe added *through June 15* under Room and Board. "But you've got to keep your end of the bargain with the cooking and cleaning and stuff."

I nodded. Mom elbowed me. "Did any of your other boyfriends give you such a good deal?" she asked.

I'd lived with three men since Dad kicked me out. None had a contract. None lived in a neighborhood where the police didn't show up weekly.

"Hold on," Joe said. "I'm not a boyfriend. This isn't a romantic thing."

"Well, not yet," Mom said. Then she leaned forward and tapped the notepad. "I want another stipulation."

"Oh my God, Mom. This is between Joe and me."

"I want to make sure you don't pop out another baby from some mystery dad."

Joe hovered the pen over the paper, gears visibly grinding. Then he wrote: *No seeing other men.*

He looked at me for confirmation.

I shrugged. "Sure." It's not like I had a line of suitors waiting.

Mom added helpfully, "You've had enough for a lifetime."

I rolled my eyes, which was apparently her cue for more meddling. She snatched the pen and wrote:

No vaping

"Mom!" I wanted to write *No meddling*, but I didn't want to start World War III.

"Audrey, the kids don't need to see your bad habits," she said. Then to Joe: "You don't smoke or vape, do you?"

"No, ma'am."

Royce stood and headed toward the entryway. "I'm gonna tell the kids outside we're moving in."

Well. I guess that settles it.

CHAPTER 13

Joe

Everyone thought I was crazy. My parents. The guys at work. A client with whom I had to cancel a Saturday golf game. Even I thought I was crazy. It was like something took over my body and started making this deal.

Griffin commented, "Make sure she gets tested for STDs before she moves in."

Try as I might to convince him the arrangement was platonic, he responded, "Yeah, right. For all you're doing for her, she had better be a housekeeper who gives happy endings. I don't know whether to be envious or fear for your demise."

Dad said, "This is the stupidest thing you've ever done. She's going to drain your bank account."

I assured him repeatedly that I would not give her access to my bank accounts or credit cards. He gifted me with a set of security cameras, "In case she tries to hock your valuables."

Mom just gave me the look that meant she was disappointed in me, as if I'd been caught using drugs, which I never have, by the way. According to Dad, she said, "I wanted him to have a woman in his life, but not this one."

Despite her misgivings, she started searching for used bedroom furniture for me on the NeighborTrade app.

On Wednesday, she found a bunk bed set for cheap, and she and Dad brought it over in his pickup. The set was in decent shape, except for the stains on one of the mattresses. I set that one out by the curb and bought a new one. Dad helped me assemble the bunks in the boys' room and only twice questioned my sanity.

Audrey's mom donated her formal dining set, a queen-size bed that the boys had been sleeping on, and the sofa and loveseat set that had been in their back family room. "I gotta get rid of them when I sell the house anyway," she said. Saturday morning, we rented a box truck to bring everything over, and Beverly had somehow convinced Liam to help. Against his wife's wishes, Audrey guessed.

"You know she's a mess, don't you?" Liam said about his sister with a tone that didn't expect an answer. "She's the reason our dad lost the shop. I give her three months, and she'll be pregnant again." Then he poked me in the chest and said, "Maybe you'll be the daddy and maybe you won't." He followed that with, "That depends on whether she's not in jail by then." He seemed to almost revel in Audrey's troubles.

* * *

Their first night as official residents was the Saturday after my invitation, the day we brought over the furniture from her mom's house.

After the kids had gone to bed, I walked through the house to admire the donated furniture that filled once-empty rooms with mish-mashed styles. Maybe mish-mash could be its own style. Someone had placed a vase of flowers in the center of the formal dining table.

I returned to find Audrey in my shower with the bathroom door wide open. Not that I could see the shower unless I went into one of the two vanity sink areas on either side of the shower and toilet room. But I needed to brush my teeth and shouldn't let her shower interrupt my schedule, right? So, I went into the vanity area. And I might have glanced into the shower room. After all, it's my house, and she didn't ask to use my shower, and she left the door wide open, probably on purpose, and the shower glass was fogged up a bit anyway…. Okay, I looked. I guess I'm a Peeping Tom. From my angle, I saw her left side, the side without tattoos. She almost looked normal. Then I came to my senses, scolded my perverted self, and turned to focus on my oral hygiene.

I heard the shower turn off, then the glass door open, and then footsteps on the tile floor. I imagined her toweling off while I concentrated on flossing.

"Hey," she said, reflected in the mirror, wearing a thin pink nightshirt and gray shorts. "I hope you didn't mind me using your shower. The other bathroom doesn't have a shower curtain."

"Oh, uh, yeah. No problem," I stammered. When I lived alone, I didn't need a curtain in the guest bath.

Her next statement caught me off guard. "I know what you're looking at."

I quickly looked down at the sink. "I…I wasn't looking at anything."

She snorted and said, "It's okay."

I glanced up again at her reflection in the mirror, fixing my gaze on her eyes. She smiled as if catching me in a lie, but not minding.

"They're nipple piercings."

Her sleepwear obviously didn't include a bra. Now that I'd been caught, I dared to glance at her chest again. Glance, not stare. It was quick enough to confirm that her two frontal protrusions didn't have the natural, rounded shape. They included two little artificial bumps on each side of her natural ones.

I looked down at the sink again, unnecessarily rinsing my toothbrush that I had rinsed only a few seconds ago. My initial glance wasn't from desire, but from noticing something out of place. Face and neck tattoos, nose rings, cheek piercings, nipple piercings.

"You got a belly button piercing, too?" I asked.

"It got infected, and I had to take it out. The hole closed over."

I didn't understand why some women did things like that to themselves. It's like they purposely tainted the places on their bodies that would most likely catch a man's eye. Was that the goal? And did I just admit that I look at women's boobs?

Maybe that's not a fair assessment of men in general. Maybe it's not all men, just those in my circle of friends. Dimitri obviously didn't mind her modifications. Men like him could overlook anything that didn't affect a woman's performance in the bedroom.

Audrey leaned in close and put her chin on my shoulder, her position removing the possibility for me to look at places I shouldn't.

"Um," she started. "Are we...?" Her voice petered off, and the corners of her mouth rose slightly in the kind of smile meant to mask an awkward moment.

I again stared at her in the mirror, waiting for her to finish her thought.

She finally whispered, "Am I sleeping with you?"

I bet she never had to ask that of the other guys she'd lived with. I'm sure they made their expectations clear from the start.

I stepped aside and turned to face her. "You're in the room with Simone, same as last time."

Her smile faded. "Oh. I thought maybe that time was 'cause Simone wasn't used to this house. And I didn't know if I should bring my toothbrush and stuff to this bathroom. Sorry." She sounded disappointed.

At the door to the hallway, she turned and quickly came back to hug me. "Good night, Joe. And thank you."

As she released me to leave, I said, "Good night, Audrey. Sweet dreams." Did I really just say sweet dreams?

CHAPTER 14

Audrey

Five days in, Joe still acted like he'd accidentally adopted a family of raccoons. Every night when I hugged him goodnight, he stiffened his back like someone had just handed him a live grenade labeled *affection*. Naturally, I planned to keep doing it forever. There's a special kind of joy in hugging a man who clearly has no idea what to do with his arms.

Thursday night – the sixth night – was my breaking point. Joe strolled in at eight-thirty like that was a perfectly reasonable hour to come home to a house full of children and one increasingly irritated woman. Every other night he'd been home between five forty-five and six fifteen, like clockwork. But tonight? Nope. Chaos.

After the kids and I finished dinner, I moved his plate from the formal dining table (which we normally used for dinner) to the kitchen table by the back door, like I was setting a trap. As soon as I heard the garage door open, I planted myself beside the table in full Angry Mom stance: arms crossed, jaw tight, eyes narrowed to slits. I was the human embodiment of *We Need to Talk*.

"Hi!" he said as he walked in.

He wasn't exactly smiling, but I watched with great satisfaction as whatever expression he *did* have slid right off his face when he saw me. His eyes dropped to the cold plate of spaghetti and meatballs like it had personally betrayed him.

"We held up eating thirty minutes waiting for you," I said, my tone as frosty as his dinner.

"You didn't have to wait up. I grabbed dinner with Griffin."

He said it so casually, like he hadn't just detonated a small emotional bomb in my kitchen.

He clearly didn't understand, so I slowed it down. "We. Waited. For. You. You've been here for dinner every other night. If you had plans, you should have let me know."

"I just figured you'd start eating at your usual time."

"What the *Helsinki*, Joe! Dinner was for *all* of us. The kids. Me. You. Believe it or not, they were excited to tell you about their day. They made new friends two blocks over and played on a Slip'n Slide. They saw ducks at the pond by the townhomes. This is big stuff in kid world!"

He held up his hands. "Okay, okay! Next time, I'll let you know ahead of time."

I picked up his plate and scraped the contents into a plastic container. "Your lunch tomorrow."

He deflated like a sad balloon. "Thanks."

"Next time, text," I added, because apparently we were covering basic communication skills now.

"Well, you could have done—" He stopped himself, probably because he saw the laser beams shooting from my eyes. "Got it. I will."

Later, after my shower, I left his room without saying goodnight. But then I turned right back around and stood in the doorway until he noticed me.

"What?" he asked, confused.

I didn't answer. I didn't smile. I just walked over, hugged him, and left.

Inside, I grinned like a villain.

Good night, Joe, I thought.

CHAPTER 15

Joe

I ran through possible defenses in my head but came up dry. Audrey had a point. I still wasn't used to this pseudo-family situation. Mark Wahlberg's character in "Instant Family" had weeks to get used to the idea of adding foster kids to their family. They had classes, meetings, and discussions. I'd jumped into the deep end of the pool while only able to dog paddle.

Wednesday night, the kids got into an argument about who started a fight that afternoon. From what I gleaned during dinnertime conversations, fights and arguments among the siblings happened a lot. I've simply been blessed not to witness any yet. So, when Audrey said the kids were eager to tell me about their day, I almost asked if they were eager to tell me about their latest fight, but I figured that wouldn't help with her current grievance.

I decided it was not the appropriate time to tell her about my Saturday game nights with friends.

* * *

As I mowed the lawn Saturday morning, Royce came out and asked if he could push the mower. If a kid was volunteering to mow the lawn for me, I was all for it. I showed him the batteries and explained the button and lever needed to start it. I gave him the warnings my dad had given me about keeping my hands and feet away from the blade.

"Those blades are nothing to fool around with," I explained. "If you need to pick up a stick or something in the way, let go of the handle, and the mower will shut off. I know a guy who lost a finger because he stuck his hand under the edge of the mower to pick up something without turning it off first."

I didn't bother to explain that the injury was from a gasoline mower that didn't have the safety features of my electric one. I just wanted Royce to respect the potential dangers.

He promised to be careful, and I let him take over. Then Colton came out and pitched a fit that Royce got special treatment. Royce elbowed Colton in the chest to keep him away from the mower. Colton got a running start and ran headlong into Royce, knocking him down. With Royce out of the way, Colton grabbed the mower handle. Fortunately, he didn't know how to restart it.

I shouted, "Colton!"

He ignored me.

Then I tried, "Royce is helping me, and you're too young. You can barely push this thing."

When he refused to let go, Royce grabbed him around his waist and wrestled him to the ground. Colton ran inside crying while Royce called after him, "Baby!"

Royce returned to the mower, expertly started it, and resumed mowing. It didn't last long because a few minutes later, Colton came from around the side of the house, dragging the water hose. He sprayed me and Royce, which actually felt good on such a hot day. But Royce abandoned his duties and chased Colton into the house. I turned off the water and finished the lawn myself.

* * *

Audrey and the kids baked cookies on Sunday to celebrate a week at their new residence. I wouldn't have associated cookie baking with a woman with a neck tattoo and a septum ring. I associate such body modifications with coffee shops and college protesters, not a homemaker mother of three. But coffee shops sell cookies, too, so what do I know? I forgot she'd made cookies for me ten years ago. Sometimes I forget she's the same person.

While Audrey monitored Colton in his bath, Simone escaped from bed and sneaked back to the kitchen. Fortunately, or unfortunately, I discovered her. She'd had an active day, and I thought she would have gone to sleep as soon as her head hit the pillow.

"You're supposed to be in bed," I pointed out.

"I need a cookie."

"It's too late for cookies. You need to go to sleep."

"Mommy said I can have a cookie." She emphasized her statement with wide eyes and a smile.

The little bugger just lied to me. "Your mother did not say that. I heard her tell you no more cookies."

The plate of cookies still sat on the counter with a covering of plastic wrap. She ignored me and reached for the plate. I picked it up and held it out of her reach.

Her face contorted into a mass of rage, and she screamed, "Give me a cookie!"

I think her eyes started glowing. I set the plate on top of the refrigerator and backed away.

She opened a lower cabinet door and slammed it shut. Pleased with the sound, she opened and slammed it again. And again. All the while saying, "Cookie!" in a voice straight out of a horror movie.

I almost shouted for Audrey to come handle her daughter, but I didn't want to give the little terror enough time to rip the door off its hinges. Instead, I grabbed her by the back of her pajama shirt and pulled her away from the cabinet. As she writhed and wriggled to get away, I kicked a chair away from the table and sat down in it, pulling her onto my lap, facing away.

When she yelled, "Let me go!" I wrapped my arms tightly around her to reduce her struggles, pinning her arms to her sides.

Her arms restrained, and her yells getting her nowhere, she bent her head down and sank her teeth into my left forearm. I wanted to scream in pain but succeeded in containing my displeasure to a low groan punctuated by deep breaths. She eventually released the bite and thrust her head back violently, hitting me in the mouth.

Eventually, after getting Colton to bed, Audrey came looking for Simone. She found me holding the sleeping tot, blood dripping down my arm, my upper lip starting to swell. Her response to the scene was, "What the *Helsinki* did you do to her?"

I recalled Audrey's addition to our agreement. *You have to let us stay for the whole school year.* School hadn't even started yet.

* * *

Monday morning at work, as I poured myself a coffee in the breakroom, I glanced at the tray of blueberry muffins sitting next to the coffee maker. A weekly gift from Debbie, one of the executive assistants. She resumed working at the firm about the same time I started, after taking several years off to raise a family. I had little professional interaction with her since she worked in another department, but seeing the muffins made me realize she might be able to help with my current situation. I went to her cubicle.

"Hi, Debbie, I need advice."

"What kind of advice, kiddo?"

"You raised, like, ten kids, right?"

She chuckled. "Eight, but sometimes I lose count. Only three are still at home."

"That means you have a lot of experience with kids, and I need some parenting advice."

"Ah. I expect going from bachelor to a house full of kids is quite a shock."

"You know about that?"

"Joe, the whole office knows about it. These walls have ears, and all of us EAs look for anything to gossip about. I think what you're doing is nuts, but I want to hear from you. What's going on?"

"The kids are out of control."

"Three of them, right?"

"Yeah. The first couple of days were fine. Then it's like they turned into different kids. Temper tantrums. Fights. Throwing stuff."

I rolled up my sleeve and showed the bite mark. "That's from the four-year-old last night. She may look like an angel, but I swear she's possessed."

"My first was an angel," Debbie said. "Even the second was pretty easy. I patted myself on the back for being a great mother with well-behaved kids, and I sneered at all those bad moms who couldn't control theirs. But then my third came along, and when he turned two, all heck broke loose. Everything I knew about parenting fell apart. Tantrums in the grocery store. Throwing food. He bit the dog. So, I know what you mean. In your case, take it as a compliment. They feel comfortable enough around you to let their guard down."

I didn't feel complimented. "But you figured it out, right? You got them to behave." If she didn't give me some encouragement, I might start pulling my hair out right in front of her.

"How old are yours?" she asked.

She said 'yours' as if they belonged to me. I answered, "Eight, five, and four."

"Those are the perfect ages for some discipline training. Look, this isn't the right setting to get into it. How's your schedule on Wednesday night?"

"I'm free."

"What about, uh…. What's the kids' mother's name?"

"Audrey."

"What about Audrey? It works best if both parents are hearing it at the same time."

Did she just call me a parent? I let it slide. "Yeah. Both of us," I said. Then I remembered the kids, the whole point of this conversation. "I'll see if she can get her mom to watch the kids. Where should we meet? Your house or a coffee shop, or something?"

"At my church. We have parenting classes on Wednesday nights. I'll meet you there at 6:30, and you can bring the kids."

"Wait. Church? I thought it would just be you imparting your wisdom on us." I started to feel tricked into going to church. I used to go with my family when I was a kid. But when I went to college, I didn't bother anymore. It didn't seem relevant.

Debbie noticed my hesitation. "Don't worry, I'll be with you, and I promise it won't be weird. I also promise it'll help you enjoy the kids more."

Not what I expected, and I'm not looking for joy, just peace. But desperate times call for desperate measures. I took a deep breath and said, "Okay. You said 6:30, right?"

She nodded. "At the south entrance. That's the side away from the freeway. I'll email you the address."

CHAPTER 16

Audrey

I was pretty sure parenting classes weren't going to teach me anything except how to sit in a circle and pretend my life was together, but honestly, I just wanted to get out of the house. My only outing in the past week had been a mile-and-a-half walk to the grocery store because we ran out of toilet paper. That's when you know you've hit rock bottom: when you're hiking for Charmin.

"My kids were just born with wild streaks," I told Joe when he suggested the class. "You're trying to fix something that can't be fixed. They came out feral."

He countered with, "Even pro athletes benefit from good coaching."

Translation: *Your parenting skills need Jesus.*

He'd already told me the kids needed to hear "no" more often. I told him they hear it plenty – they just treat it like background noise.

As we were getting ready to leave, Joe stopped me and said, "What if you left the, uh…" He pointed under his nose, then at each cheek. "The piercings at home?"

Instant regret for agreeing to this outing. "You're embarrassed to walk into a church with me, aren't you? I'm too much of a freak for church, right?"

His eyes went wide like I'd accused him of kicking puppies. "No! That's not it. I just thought you might want…."

I dragged my hand across my neck tattoo. "Maybe I should take this off too."

"No. I mean… I thought… Never mind."

He looked so pitiful – no longer the puppy kicker but the puppy who itself who knows he chewed up your shoes – that I didn't cancel. If the church people couldn't handle my piercings, that was their problem.

Debbie, the woman from Joe's work, met us in the lobby. The building looked less like a church and more like a corporate headquarters for Jesus, Inc. If this wasn't a mega church, then I didn't know what qualified.

"Audrey, it's so good to meet you," she said before Joe even introduced us.

Then she looked at my kids and said, "You must be the awesome kids Joe told me about."

Awesome? Joe had never used that word around me. Around me, he used words like "uncontrollable" and "exhausting."

After she took the kids to their classes – promising they'd have fun, which I doubted – she led us to a room with five other couples already waiting.

"Sorry I'm late," she said, dropping her tote bag on a table. "Guys, this is Audrey and Joe. They're here to see if what we're selling works."

"It's only been two weeks, and I'm already seeing a difference," a man said.

"In him and the kids," his wife added, earning chuckles.

Debbie handed Joe a book. "Sit anywhere."

The room looked like it doubled as a Sunday morning indoctrination —er, Bible study – classroom. We sat in the empty third row.

I leaned over. "You didn't tell me Debbie was the teacher."

"I didn't know," he whispered back.

Debbie wrote on the whiteboard: *No talking. No emotions.*

I bristled. "Sorry," I muttered, assuming we'd already been scolded.

"Oh!" Debbie said. "No, that's not for class." She smiled apologetically. "In here, I want you to talk, ask questions, make comments."

A mom in the front row pointed at the board. "That's our mantra for disciplining the kids. No talking. No emotions. No lecturing. No yelling."

"Thanks, Amy," Debbie said. Then to us: "I'll bring you up to speed after class. It's also in the book."

As the lesson went on, I realized my kids weren't the worst. One mom described her son throwing tantrums in stores until she bought him whatever he wanted. I didn't have that problem because I can't buy things when I have no money.

Then there was Nolan, who punched holes in walls during tantrums, and Kasey, whose favorite phrase was "I hate you," a verbal grenade that she apparently deployed frequently.

I nudged Joe. "See? This is normal kid behavior."

Right then another mom said, "But her sister Gemma is so sweet."

"Yeah," Gemma's mom added. "It's hard to believe they grew up in the same house."

Okay, maybe not *completely* normal.

Still, hearing other parents' war stories was refreshing. I didn't want to admit Joe was right about the class, but I was already planning to come back.

And best of all? Not a single person blinked at my piercings or tattoos.

Miracles do happen in church.

CHAPTER 17

Joe

As Audrey and I walked to the children's wing to pick up the kids after class, I asked, "So, what did you think?"

She shrugged. "It sounds too good to be true. But at least Debbie didn't try to beat us over our heads with her Bible."

With ten more months to go in my commitment to house Audrey, I was ready to try anything that might get her kids under control. If Debbie had suggested sacrificing a chicken on the church altar, I'd have headed to the poultry farm. What I heard in the class provided hope that life didn't have to be so miserable.

"It doesn't hurt to try it," I said.

"Okay," she said. "But you've got to back me up."

"I will," I promised. Darn right I will; my life is on the line.

The kids, too, were more agreeable than I expected. Maybe they also looked forward to a break from the monotony of the house. When we picked them up, the younger ones presented us with macaroni and yarn bracelets and hand-colored drawings of Biblical scenes.

When we pressed them for their take, Royce shrugged his shoulders and said, "It was okay."

Colton asked, "Can we come back?"

Simone echoed Colton. "Yeah, can we come back?"

That clinched the deal. We would be back for more of Debbie's wisdom. And the possibility of peace at home.

CHAPTER 18

Audrey

Joe waited with us at the corner for the school bus, looking like a man who had accidentally wandered into a neighborhood festival he didn't remember RSVPing to. We were surrounded by other parents who were also ready – *eager*, even – to ship their children off for the first day of school. Royce acted like this was just another Monday, but Colton grinned so wide you'd think he was about to board a roller coaster at Six Flags instead of a bus with sticky seats and questionable smells. Meanwhile, Simone was devastated that she couldn't join her brothers on their grand voyage into academia.

When the yellow bus rounded the corner, one of the kids yelled, "Here it comes!" which triggered a chorus of cheers from the younger ones, as if the bus contained a celebrity arriving on the red carpet.

A girl who looked about ten or eleven rolled her eyes and said, "Calm down. It's just a bus." Every neighborhood has at least one preteen who's already over everything.

Colton and Royce adjusted their backpacks and rushed to the curb as if the bus driver might peel out without them. Simone tried to bolt after them, but I caught her arm just in time. That child would absolutely stow away if given half a chance.

Joe swooped in, lifted her onto his shoulders, and suddenly she was fine – because apparently being tall fixes everything. I glanced at his bare forearm; the bite mark she'd given him had already faded. Small mercies.

"You didn't have to come out here," I told him.

"They seemed so excited it rubbed off on me," he said. "Plus, it's a good chance to meet more neighbors."

Translation: *I'm trying to look normal in front of the community.*

We stood with the other parents, waving like we were sending the boys off to war instead of second grade. Once the bus turned the corner and disappeared, Joe lifted Simone off his shoulders—then immediately flipped her upside down and carried her into the house like a giggling sack of potatoes.

He left for work right after that, probably relieved to go somewhere where no one bites him or tries to sneak onto public transportation.

* * *

Joe missed their return in the afternoon, but they made sure to fill him in on their adventures over dinner.

Colton looked serious as he said, "There are so many kids at school."

Joe tried to stifle a laugh, which prompted Colton to ask, "Why are you laughing?"

Joe ignored the question and asked, "Did you make any new friends?"

"Most of the kids are okay," Royce said, trying to sound cool. "I already met a couple of them from the neighborhood. A boy from that church is in my class. He gave me a pencil."

"Was that the highlight of the day?" Joe asked. Royce didn't catch Joe's subtle sarcasm.

Colton stretched his left hand across the table toward Joe. "A girl gave me a tattoo," he announced.

A press-on tattoo of a pink dinosaur adorned the back of his hand. I'd already heard this story, but Colton seemed eager to tell it again.

Royce sneered and said, "It's a girl tattoo." I'd already heard that one, too.

"Is not!" Colton yelled back. "It's a dinosaur. Dinosaurs are for boys."

"It's pink. That's a girl color," Royce insisted.

Joe took Colton's hand in his and leaned forward for a better look. "I like it. Did you do it at school or wait till you got home?"

Colton beamed at the affirmation. "At school. Lily put the paper in her mouth to get it wet, then she put it on my hand and rubbed it."

Joe glanced at me, then back at Colton. "So, Lily mixed it with her spit and then held your hand. I think you might have to marry her now."

Simone's eyes got wide. "Colton's gonna get married? He's just a kid."

Colton gave Joe and Simone a look of disgust and muttered, "Y'all are stupid."

As much as I wanted to laugh, I felt I had to jump in as a mother and call out, "Hey! We don't use that word! No one's stupid here."

"Lily gave tattoos to other kids, too," Colton said.

Royce jumped off his seat and said, "I'll be back."

He returned a few seconds later with his new pencil, presenting it as if it were a prized possession. It was the kind given away by businesses with their company name and logo. This one had a light gray shaft with red lettering.

"Flynn gave me this. He said it's for a club he's in."

"I've got a pencil sharpener around here somewhere," Joe said, taking the pencil from Royce. He turned it to read the inscription. "Boys in Action."

Royce explained, "Flynn said it's a club that goes camping and teaches you how to save people and stuff."

I'd already heard that when he got home from school. That's when he asked if he could join.

"Flynn said I should join. Momma said she'd have to think about it."

I looked up the organization. It sounded fun, and I wouldn't mind the boys focusing their energy on something positive. But it costs money to join and to do many of the activities. And I've got two boys, which means double the cost.

"Yeah, that's a big commitment," Joe said. "Meetings every week, uniforms, supplies, and equipment."

He handed the pencil back to Royce and said, "Go check the second drawer of my desk. I think that's where I put the pencil sharpener." I couldn't tell if Joe was legitimately trying to be helpful or low-level mocking Royce's obsession with a pencil.

When Royce left the room, Joe said, "It's not a bad idea. I did Cub Scouts when I was a kid. This kind of thing might help with behavior. For both boys."

I wish he hadn't said that in front of Colton. "You know I can't afford it."

"I can," he said.

CHAPTER 19

Joe

At first, when we started doing the one-two-three count for their misbehavior, the kids ignored us. At the next parenting class, Debbie and other parents warned us that a little rebellion was normal; just stick with the program. Give a warning count, minimize talking, and control your emotions. Meting out discipline mostly fell to Audrey, but when the kids finally figured out that she and I were on the same page and that by the count of three they would end up in a time-out or have some other consequence, they started getting their act together. Only once did I have to carry a kid to his bedroom for a time-out. Audrey said she only had to hold their bedroom doors shut a couple of times before they realized we were serious about the time-outs.

The highlight for me was when Colton sat in Simone's usual spot at the table, and Simone threatened to hit him. Audrey held up a finger as taught in the parenting class and said, "That's one."

Simone had been irritable since the boys started school. I don't know if she missed her brothers or was envious that they got to go to school and she didn't. I only know that she had a little relapse in the discipline plan.

Simone picked up Colton's plate and acted as if she were about to drop it on the floor. Audrey held up a second finger. "Two."

Simone put the plate back on the table, came to me, and said, "Squeeze me." Then she turned around and backed into my legs.

I wasn't quite sure if I heard correctly. "What?"

"Squeeze me before I do something bad."

I picked her up, set her on my lap, and wrapped my arms tightly around her as I'd done after her tantrum in the kitchen a few weeks back. I silently prayed she wouldn't bite me this time and remembered to tilt my head to the side to avoid another reverse head butt.

After a couple of minutes and no bites, I whispered, "Are you better now?"

She nodded and whispered back, "Yes."

I released her, and she hopped down and took her seat in the place that used to be Colton's.

Audrey looked at me with knitted brow. "What was that?"

I shrugged. "I'm learning to tame the dragon."

CHAPTER 20

Audrey

Joe came into the kitchen after the kids finished breakfast, collecting their plates like a man who had accepted his fate as Household Busboy.

I gave him my brightest, chirpiest, borderline-suspicious "Good morning" as I set down plates of bacon and scrambled eggs for the two of us.

"Morning," he said, taking a heroic swig of orange juice before absolutely burying his eggs under a blizzard of black pepper. I'm talking *visibility-zero conditions*.

Right before taking a bite, he said, "Hey, uh, at least once a month, usually on a Saturday night, I hang out with friends."

"Um hmm," I said, picking up a slice of bacon with my fingers.

He continued, "Sometimes we go to Dave and Buster's. Sometimes we go to someone's apartment for games. We mix it up."

I waited. There was a conjunction coming. I could feel it. The *and* or *but* was hovering in the air like a mosquito.

He skipped it. "I missed the last one because of moving you in."

Ah. So, the conjunction was just fashionably late.

"And, well, I, uh, want to join them this time," he finally said.

There it was. *And.* The truth always arrives eventually.

Then he tacked on, "I don't think you'd be interested, but you can come if you want." The tone was pure afterthought – like when a waiter asks if you want dessert but clearly hopes you'll say no.

"Tonight," I said. Not a question. A diagnosis.

"Yeah, tonight. Kelli said you're welcome to come. We're doing games at her apartment."

I didn't know Kelli, and in that moment, I didn't care if she was a saint or a serial killer. "When did Kelli say that?"

Instead of answering, he shoved an entire slice of bacon into his mouth like it was a defensive maneuver.

"Don't you think it would've been nice to give me a few days' notice?" I asked.

I stared at him while he chewed. And chewed. And chewed. Finally, he swallowed and said, "I wasn't sure you'd like that sort of thing anyway."

He winced as he said it, like even *he* knew it sounded like a flaming pile of nonsense. Did he forget we used to play games with friends at his house in high school? Did he think I'd suddenly become allergic to fun?

"You know," I said, "one way to be sure is to ask."

I kept staring, wondering how I fit into his life, wondering what he told his friends about me, wondering if he ever thought I might like a break from refereeing small humans.

He offered a limp, "I'm sorry."

My mother once explained the stereotype about girls with tattoos and piercings – as if I hadn't lived it. According to her, people like me hang out in smoke-filled pool halls with bearded bikers or sit in dingy apartments getting high on weed and mushrooms. Never mind that my wildest night lately involved folding laundry at 11 p.m.

Joe had never once asked about my friends or what I liked to do for fun. In that moment, I felt less like a roommate and more like a charity project he didn't want to introduce to the donors.

"I can't get a babysitter on such short notice," I said. "My mom would refuse simply on principle." I'm sure he hadn't thought about the kids at all. Men rarely do when planning "fun."

Another "I'm sorry," followed by, "I should have told you several days ago." His sincerity ticked up from 3% to maybe 7%.

"Go ahead without me," I said. If I didn't sound sincere, good. I wasn't.

"You don't mind?"

Are all men so *Finland* clueless? "Why would I mind?" I said. "You had a life before we showed up. I get it. We shouldn't get in the way of that."

Yet, I thought, now that we're here… shouldn't we get in the way?

He finished his breakfast in silence, then escaped outside to mow the lawn like it was a national emergency.

CHAPTER 21

Joe

None of my friends in the game night group had kids, and none were married. But two couples had been dating for a while. When I explained to the group why I hadn't brought Audrey, the couples exchanged knowing glances and clicked their tongues.

"I just don't think she's the kind of person who'd be into board games," I defended.

"You screwed up," one of the women scolded.

"How?" I asked. "Audrey's not my girlfriend. She just lives with me."

Another girl said, "You've got a lot to learn about women. You may need to stop for flowers or candy tonight."

"We're not dating!"

"That's beside the point," the first one said.

The male partners of the couples shook their heads in pity. The single guys joined my confusion.

* * *

I got back at 11:30, not late by Saturday night standards. The back porch light was on, but the lights inside were off. I tried to be quiet as I closed the back door behind me. My phone's light helped me navigate through the dark house when I heard a hiss. Startled, I dropped the phone. I quickly picked it up and shone it around the room. Audrey sat on the sofa, looking somewhat ominous in the dim phone light.

"Dang! You scared the crap out of me!" I said in a whisper.

She asked, "Do you believe in God?" Her question only added to her scary, shadowed appearance. Was she thinking of sending me off to meet him? I looked at her hands for a knife or a ninja throwing star. She held only a phone and a tissue. When she sniffled, I realized that was what I had earlier mistaken for a hiss.

"Yeah," I answered in the tentative voice that I used if I wasn't sure I liked where the conversation was going.

"You used to go to church, but you don't anymore," she said. "Why did you stop?"

"I don't know. I went off to college and just got distracted with other things. Why?"

She sniffled again and said, "I want to go to church tomorrow."

That came out of nowhere. I don't think either of us had been to church in years before the parenting class. We hadn't even talked about it.

"Okay," I said. Since I didn't take her to the game night, the least I could do was take her to church.

She pressed a tissue to her eyes.

"Are you alright?" I asked.

"Yeah. No. I don't know. I'm with the kids all day, every day. One thing I got from Debbie's class was how nice it was to have a little break from them and have adult conversations, even if just for an hour or two."

"I'm sorry," I said. "I should have told you about the game night days ago. Then maybe you could have gotten your mother to babysit."

"That's okay. You have your life. I have mine."

Her voice was softer than the sarcastic tone from this morning. Since she still hadn't gotten up from the sofa, I sat down beside her. Her phone slipped off her lap and into the gap between us. When I picked it up to hand it back, I noticed the screen was open to a video about prison life.

"And my life sucks," she added.

After the scolding from my friends, I offered, "Maybe sometime I can watch the kids, and you can go out with your friends."

"Joe," she paused to dab the tissue to her eyes again, "you're it. You're my only friend."

I hoped that wasn't true. I may have given her a place to stay, but I haven't been much of a friend. I talk to the kids more than to her. "Oh, come on. Girls always have lots of friends. What about the cousin you went to Europe with?"

She gave a little grunt. "We're too different. I haven't talked much with Lainey since Europe. I came back knocked up, while she came back and found Mr. Perfect, had perfect kids, and lives a perfect life."

She rested her head on my shoulder before whispering, "I'm sorry for dumping my crap on you."

I tried to ignore the prick of her pointed dimple piercing in my shoulder and tried to find something comforting to say. The best I could come up with was, "Things will get better."

CHAPTER 22

Audrey

I hoped Joe's prediction about things getting better would come true, but honestly, I was skeptical. Back in our previous life together, he was the one who analyzed every detail like he was running a NASA launch simulation. I was the optimistic one – the human equivalent of a car with bald tires on an icy road, speeding toward a curve while yelling, "It'll be fine!" right before reality slapped me across the face.

And then there was Lainey.

I hadn't talked to her in years, mostly because I credit her with launching my slide into what I now lovingly call my *European Slut Era*. I didn't go to Europe planning to sleep with a different guy in every city – that was her itinerary. I used to think she was edgy and fun. At one point, I even wanted to be like her. That was before I realized "edgy and fun" was code for "makes terrible decisions with confidence."

Had I known her hookup plans, I wouldn't have gone. I only went because… honestly, I don't even know. Some rebellious part of me wanted to prove to my dad that forcing me to break up with Joe would cost him a boatload of money and wouldn't guarantee I wouldn't run right back to Joe later. Spoiler: it didn't.

Then Lainey pimped me out to a random Swedish guy in London so she could hook up with his friend.

"He's hot," she said about the Swede. "If I hadn't met his friend first, I'd take him myself."

Ah yes, the endorsement every girl dreams of.

After a dinner involving several bottles of wine – because apparently that was our new personality – we went back to their tiny flat. Before disappearing into the bedroom with her guy, she told me, "Live a little," then turned to my guy and said, "Be gentle, she's inexperienced."

Then she popped back out, slapped two condoms on the table like she was dealing poker cards, and vanished again.

Stieg – pretty sure that was his name – smiled and poured me more wine. The night on the sofa with him was awkward, uncomfortable, and about as sexy as a dental cleaning. Afterward, I wanted to scrub my skin off. I imagined Joe looking at me with disappointment, and I felt the tether connecting me to my safe life back home fraying.

I told Lainey how uneasy I felt. Her response was basically the European version of "What happens in Vegas stays in Vegas."

Except it didn't.

With every encounter – always encouraged by Lainey – my inhibitions fell away piece by piece. But instead of feeling liberated, I felt like I was auditioning for a role I didn't want. Like I was trying to win Lainey's approval or convince myself that this was what modern, empowered women did.

Lainey eventually left her ho phase behind.

I returned pregnant.

Simone interrupted my spiraling thoughts with a soft, "Mommy?"

Joe patted my leg, and we both stood.

"Church tomorrow," I reminded him. "I'll wake you up at eight."

CHAPTER 23

Joe

Audrey wore a pale blue dress to church; the first time I'd seen her in a dress. At least, the first time since high school. I didn't even know she had one. And her hair was down. I can't remember if she'd worn it down since our reunion at the coffee shop several weeks ago. She usually pulled it into a ponytail. The hair framing her face and neck lessened the impact of the giant lotus design and facial accessories, softening the look. At least it did for me.

I'd become used to her body art over the last few weeks but became more aware of it as we made our way to the Sunday School class that one of the parenting class couples invited us to. As we walked through the hallway after dropping the kids off at their classes and crossing paths with people arriving for the early worship service, I caught a few older women eyeing her up and down and then whispering something to a husband or companion. If Audrey noticed, she didn't say anything.

A call of "Audrey!" had us looking around for the source. The sea of people parted, revealing Emma from our parenting class, who said, "You're looking pretty. I love your dress."

Her husband, Lucas, asked me, "Are you coming to check out our Sunday School class?"

"Yeah," I said. "We didn't know where to go, so we just started following some of the parents from the kids' area. And now we've found you. Or you found us."

The women started walking, not waiting for us, and it looked like Audrey had already started getting her adult conversation. In the classroom, other women joined Audrey and Emma. The few words we guys exchanged centered around baseball, but the women seemed to be learning everything there was to know about each other's kids. Names, ages, and how they handled the transition from summer vacation to school. The conversation continued until someone said, "Welcome," loudly enough to be heard over the buzz. That was the signal to find a seat.

After class, we followed Emma and Lucas to the worship service. Audrey didn't find the message nearly as interesting as the discussions with the women. When the preacher wrapped up his sermon and called for the congregation to stand, I nudged her awake.

"Did you get your fill of adult conversation?" I teased, as we headed to the children's wing to get the kids.

"No."

"No?" That was a surprise.

"No," she reiterated. "That's why we're meeting some of the families at Cici's Pizza for lunch."

"Oh, really?"

"Yeah. And you're paying."

"For everyone?"

"Just us," she assured. Then she touched my arm and looked up at me with big puppy eyes and drew out, "Pleeeaaase," with her mouth stretched wide in a begging smile.

For a moment, I saw the adorably cute face from long ago smiling from behind the piercings, and I smiled at that brief glimpse of what was.

"Sure," I said. "My family used to go to Cici's Pizza a couple of times a month when I was a kid. I don't know anywhere else that has an all-you-can-eat pizza buffet." I didn't mind the adult conversation, either.

CHAPTER 24

Audrey

After getting the kids to bed, I tapped on Joe's door and poked my head in. He sat at his thrift-store desk – the one he wedged between his bed and the wall, creating an office out of pure stubbornness. He said he used to work at the kitchen table, but once we moved in, he retreated to this little corner, his new hermit headquarters.

He swiveled toward me. "Shower time?"

That had become our nightly ritual. After weeks of living here, we still hadn't gotten a shower curtain for the kids' bathroom, which was starting to feel less like a bathroom and more like a water-hazard obstacle course. So, every night, after tucking the kids in, I'd tap on Joe's door – just in case he was picking his nose or doing something equally tragic – and then march straight through his room to his shower. We never discussed it. I just did it. He never objected. That's basically a contract.

Even if the kids' bathroom had a shower curtain, I'd still prefer Joe's shower. Not just because it's nicer, but because it's *his*. Sometimes I feel like a live-in maid. But walking through the master bedroom and using the master shower – while he knows I'm doing it – makes me feel less like a servant and more like I'm part of his world.

Of course, the same could be said of a golden retriever. Except dogs don't use showers. But they do trot through master bedrooms with the same hopeful energy I apparently have.

Sometimes I leave the bathroom door open on purpose, but he's never peeked in. Not once. I almost wish he would. It would be proof he still had a tiny spark of interest left from the old days. A flicker. A pilot light. *Something.*

But tonight, instead of heading to the bathroom, I walked straight to him. Because sometimes the golden retriever wants attention.

"Can I talk to you about something?"

"Sure," he said. "What's up?"

Though we were living together for the past several weeks, the only deep discussions we had were about the parenting class and its effect on the kids. Most evenings after dinner, he either watched baseball on TV or went to his bedroom to work on his computer.

I sat on the edge of the bed next to his chair. "I talked to the lawyer on Friday. A new one in Beaumont." Then I paused, trying to decide which emotions I would let through: anger, fear, humiliation.

"Friday? Why didn't you tell me then?"

I shrugged. "You were busy. I was busy." He had been on the phone with some chick planning what sounded like a date. I later found out they were discussing Saturday's game night.

"Well, what did he say?" Joe asked.

I decided to go with a neutral tone. "She. She said they're reducing my charges from felony to Class A misdemeanor because the van wasn't worth as much as Dimitri reported."

"That's great!" he said, with more enthusiasm than I felt. "Does that mean you only have to do community service?"

I glanced down before saying, "No." Then I decided I should look at him for the next part. "She said they still want jail time."

His enthusiasm evaporated. "Why?"

"Because I stole the van," I said in a tone that questioned why Joe didn't get it. "The DA wants to look tough on crime."

"So, what now?"

"The trial is set for October 9th, which we already knew. They're offering a plea deal of thirty days. But if it goes to trial, she said I could get a year."

"Or you could get nothing," he said optimistically. "If they find you didn't really steal it, that you were only late on payments, you could get off completely."

I sighed before explaining, "It's a big gamble. She said that's very unlikely."

"What about the fact that Dimitri was…. You know, the alternative payment method. He's a slimeball. He took advantage of you, exploited your poverty. Shouldn't that matter?"

"He would just deny it, then it becomes a 'he-said, she-said' thing."

"I heard what he said," Joe said. "I can testify about the arrangement."

"They'll say Dimitri was joking, or that you misheard him, or that you're too involved with me to be a reliable witness."

He got out, "But…," before I cut him off. I appreciated his desire to help, but I knew it would be of no use.

"Joe, don't pull yourself into this," I told him. "The lawyer said she'd talk to her partners, but bringing that up could make me look worse. Questionable morals. Poor decisions. Basically, my greatest hits."

He went quiet for a couple of seconds, then said, "I'm sorry."

I stood up, trying to form a sentence. "I, uh… I…." Nothing. My brain had left the chat.

He stood up too. "What is it? Just tell me."

I closed my eyes, turned around, and backed into him. "I need a squeeze. Like you did for Simone the other day."

"Like I used to do with us," he said.

I nodded, and his arms wrapped around me, pulling me tight against his chest – tighter than a hug, not quite a Heimlich maneuver, but close. Strong enough to immobilize me if I tried to wriggle away. It had been so long I'd almost forgotten. Back then, whenever I spiraled, he'd hold me from behind until I calmed down. The first couple of times, I fought it like a feral cat. The very first time, I'd yelled at him to leave. Instead, he held on – silent, steady, annoyingly correct. After that, I learned to just ride it out.

I'd forgotten all about those tight hugs until Simone asked for one and he did it without hesitation. Kids always know the good stuff before adults do.

The storm in my head started to settle, and my shoulders dropped. Joe loosened his grip.

"Not yet," I whispered, grabbing his forearms to keep them in place. I needed a few more minutes of being emotionally bubble-wrapped.

Eventually, I let go and headed to the shower. When I finished and stood at the sink brushing my teeth, he watched me from his desk chair with pity in his eyes – like I was a sad documentary animal he wasn't sure how to help.

I finished up and crossed through his bedroom to go back to mine. He met me at the door.

"Isn't there anything I can do to help?" he asked.

His concern made me smile. "It's still a few weeks away," I said.

I wrapped my arms around him for our nightly hug – the regular kind, not the industrial-strength squeeze – and whispered, "When I'm gone, will you take care of the kids?"

He patted my back. "Of course." And honestly? His hugs haven't been stiff lately.

CHAPTER 25

Joe

Dad pulled the rope to lower the folding ladder leading to the attic of the garage. With the ladder unfolded and ready for climbing, he motioned for me to proceed.

As I climbed, he asked, "Are you doing this of your own free will?"

"You think I'm being held hostage or blackmailed or something?"

"Yeah. They're not your kids, and you claim Audrey's not your girlfriend. If she were, I might understand, since men do crazy things to win a girl's favor. What you're doing just doesn't make sense."

He remained at the bottom of the ladder while I rummaged around the attic for storage trunks with my name on them. I moved boxes of Christmas ornaments and finally found one.

"Which part?" I asked. "Camping with kids or the whole Boys in Action thing?"

"Letting them live with you rent-free. Taking her boys to Scouts. Everything."

"Not Scouts, Boys in Action."

I popped the clasps on the trunk and raised the lid. It was a time capsule from fifteen years ago. Camp stove, cooking utensils, aluminum cookware, and enameled bowls, plates, and cups. I doubt camping technology has changed much.

"Knock-off Scouts," Dad said. "Two months ago, you acted like they were moving in against your will. Now you're taking them camping."

"I only found one trunk," I called down. "You sure the other one's up here?"

"You're the one who put them up there."

"Like a million years ago," I said. I moved more junk that should have been thrown away. "Found it."

This second trunk contained a lantern, a two-person dome tent, and a box of oxidizing hand warmers.

I called down, "Where's the big family tent?"

"You mean the one you took to Lake Buchanan back when you were in college? The one your friends ruined?"

I forgot about the damage on that trip. After my buddies broke two of the fiberglass poles and burned a hole in the side when they lit the aerosol bug repellent on fire, I threw the tent in the park's dumpster. That's what happens when you mix beer, frat brothers, and camping.

I dragged the trunks down the ladder, and Dad helped me get them into the car, one in the trunk – a trunk in the trunk – and the other in the back seat.

Mom came out to check on us. "I found three sleeping bags, but they smell a little musty. I put them on the sofa. Wash them before you use them. I think your sister took hers with her."

Dad was right. I was crazy. Maybe I was too much of a pushover. Or maybe I saw kids who've been deprived of a decent childhood and felt sorry for them. It was hard to say no to kids who looked at me with pleading eyes. If I were willing to volunteer at the Waller Children's Home during my firm's community outreach program, shouldn't I be willing to help needy kids in my own house? And take them camping?

* * *

The way the kids reacted to going camping, people would think we were going to Disneyland. The whole Boys in Action local chapter was going, not just Royce's and Colton's crews, which were what they called the small groups of six to eight boys. The chapter leaders encouraged the entire family to participate, which pleased Simone to no end. When Audrey signed up Royce and Colton for BIA, Simone thought she would be a Trail Boy, too. Or maybe that would be Trail Girl. She pouted the whole time we sat through that first meeting. Audrey assured her she could join the girls' program next year.

Some of the families arrived at the campsite early and had their tents set up before we got there. According to the crew chiefs, each crew tried to set up their tents near each other at the campsite. That didn't work for us. We almost bought two tents, one for Colton's crew and another for Royce's. But then we got into an argument about which of us adults would stay with which boy. When I said we, I meant Colton and Royce.

Since the boys were of different ages, they were assigned to different crews. At the crew meetings, Audrey and I switched off each week with which boy we would take. But Colton and Royce each insisted on staying in my tent on the campout. That led to the argument at the sporting goods store. Both boys wanted to be in my tent, which Royce called the Men's Tent. While Simone had no problem with that, Audrey seemed irritated at being rejected.

We ended up getting a large two-room family tent. One room for the boys and me, and the other for Audrey and Simone.

"At least one of my kids doesn't mind staying with me," she grumbled.

We also bought cots for the kids, the old wood and canvas kind that had space underneath to store gear and duffel bags. Audrey and I would each use an air mattress.

CHAPTER 26

Audrey

The BIA chapter had multiple crews, each with its own designated campsite, tiny, semi-organized tribal villages of parents, kids, and questionable packing decisions. Families with kids in different crews could pick whichever campsite they wanted, which felt very *choose your own adventure*, but with more bug spray. We set up our tent with Royce's crew mostly because one of the dads had hauled some of our overflow gear that wouldn't fit in the trunk of Joe's Camry. Bless that man and his truck bed.

Joe had taken off work early so we could get everything set up before sunset. Most families had done the same. Then a late arrival pulled up in a tiny sedan.

"They're going to be pitching their tent in the dark," I said to the group of adults arranging firewood like they were preparing for a Viking funeral.

Mark, the crew chief, called out, "Boys! Go help Ethan and his mom unload their car."

Lina stepped out – single mom of two, one boy in Royce's crew and a girl Colton's age. I didn't know if she was divorced or never married. She'd mentioned her kids spent weekends with their dad, so he existed, just not in the Boys in Action universe.

"Maybe I should help her set up," Joe said, already taking a step toward her campsite.

"You're too slow," I said, nodding toward the two men who had sprinted over like volunteers at a charity marathon.

Lina was… well, she was *Lina*. Light brown hair, slender build, Daisy Duke shorts, and a white tie-front blouse showing just enough midriff to make the dads suddenly remember they had core muscles. Meanwhile, I was rocking the "sloppy mom goes camping" aesthetic: baggy T-shirt, roomy shorts, and zero intention of impressing anyone.

The boys unloaded her gear in a pile and then stood there waiting for instructions like tiny, eager employees. After quick hugs between Lina and the two men – yes, hugs – one of them said, "Guys, why don't y'all show Ethan around the campground?"

The boys practically dragged Ethan away to show him the local attractions: the lake and the restrooms. Truly, the height of luxury.

One dad unfolded a tarp. The other pulled out her tent. Both were single dads, and I had a strong suspicion they appreciated her "style" just as much as Joe did.

* * *

The main events happened on Saturday. Each crew had an assignment, some on meal duty, some on cleanup. Training included knot tying and first aid. Each crew also had its own fun activities, such as hiking and swimming. Some of the older boys taught the rest of the chapter about water safety, guided by the adult crew chiefs. Then they took turns canoeing and swimming.

I recognized a few parents from church whose kids were in other crews. We nodded to each other.

And of course, the boys did typical boy things. Colton caught a lizard and threw it at Simone while the rest of his crew looked on and laughed. Simone screamed and chased the boys with fists full of dirt, trying to throw it at them. She missed, which only added to her anger. I didn't even have to use my newly learned discipline techniques as Colton's crew chief and the chapter leader stepped in and scolded Colton and the other boys for teasing and misbehaving. They emphasized that one of the missions of Boys in Action is to help people.

"Throwing reptiles at people is not helping them," his crew chief said.

"She's my sister," Colton said, as if that made a difference.

"That especially goes for sisters and mothers," the chapter leader noted.

I couldn't help but smile and silently yell, *Thank you, thank you, thank you.* I said it out loud to those leaders privately.

* * *

Since our daughters were close in age, Lina and I took them to a playground about half a mile up the park road. A couple of other moms were already there with their non-BIA kids, all of them looking like they'd escaped their campsites for a brief moment of sanity.

"Your kids call Joe by his name," Lina observed. "Is he their stepdad?"

I paused, trying to decide which version of the truth would sound least unhinged. Rent-a-Dad? No, that implied a financial transaction. Government-issued father figure? Honestly, more believable than reality. Or maybe I should've said he was my boss, and I blackmailed him into taking my kids camping. That would've been fun just to watch the other moms' faces.

But the truth is easier to remember. "No. He's a friend who helps me take care of them."

Lina frowned. "Just a friend? Not a boyfriend?"

I knew this was going to be a hard sell. "Just a friend. I mean, we dated ten years ago, but then life happened. Long story. We moved in with him over the summer, so the kids are around him all the time."

"So, none of your kids are his?"

Was this a conversation or an interrogation?

"Sounds like a big brother," she said. "The kind I wish I had."

One of the other moms, who had clearly been eavesdropping, chimed in. "Sounds like father material to me."

Lina sighed. "I wish my kids' father was as attentive as Joe. Luke acts like they're an interruption to his life."

I thought about Joe. We *were* an interruption to his life. The man turned down golf with a client to be here. That's practically a marriage proposal in dad-world.

Just then, a mom yelled, "Eric, come back here!"

We turned to see a toddler marching toward a row of dumpsters like he was on a mission.

"That's one!" she shouted.

The boy paused, looked back, then took another step toward the trash.

"That's two!"

He ignored her completely and sprinted to the swing set. She jogged after him and immediately started pushing him like nothing had happened. No lecture. No consequences. Just… swing time. Had she been through Debbie's class?

"My kids behave better now that Joe's around." I hadn't meant to say that out loud. It just slipped out like a confession at church.

The eavesdropping mom jumped back in. "I don't know your Joe, but you'd better snatch him up before someone else does."

It's not that I hadn't tried. I'd hinted. I'd shown appreciation. I'd orchestrated family dinners like a woman running a psychological experiment. And still, Joe treated me like a sibling he didn't quite trust with the remote.

I wanted to tell them all to mind their own business, but instead I said, "I don't think I'm his type anymore."

That should've ended it, but Lina asked, "Wait – he doesn't already have a girlfriend, does he?"

I considered asking if she wanted to submit an application, but sarcasm can be dangerous around moms who wear Daisy Dukes unironically. "No. No girlfriend."

I braced myself for someone to ask if he was gay. Miraculously, no one did.

We all walked back to the campsite together. One mom said, "The next campout's at Huntsville. I like that park better. They have a snack bar if you need to sneak a treat away from the boys."

"And the restrooms are nicer," another added. "At least they were last year."

The first mom decided to take a poll. "Who's going to Huntsville?"

I tried to stay quiet, but eventually they all looked at me. "I'll have to skip the next one. I'll be out of town."

Simone, my precious little traitor, announced, "We can't go 'cause Mommy's going to jail."

Conversation: dead. Moms: staring. Me: considering faking my own death.

"That's enough, Simone," I growled.

She disagreed. "The police took her to jail last time, but then they let her go, and now she has to go back."

I wanted to put her in time-out until college, but the counting method wasn't going to save me here.

After a long, painful pause, one mom asked, "Is any of that true?"

A knot formed in my stomach. I nodded. "I missed some car payments, and it got out of hand."

"She stole our van," Simone added helpfully. "'Cause it was really Mr. Dimitri's van."

My face was so hot I could've roasted a marshmallow on it. "It was a misunderstanding, and I didn't have money for a good lawyer," I said. Half-truth, but better than the whole mess.

Lina suddenly said, "Has anyone seen Hayley?"

Bless her.

"Simone, have you seen Hayley?" I asked.

"No."

We hurried back to camp and found Hayley and several boys staring up at a tree near the chuck box.

"Mommy, look!" Colton said.

A raccoon sat on a branch, holding a bag of marshmallows like it had just won the lottery.

I smiled, grateful that, for once, a raccoon had better timing than my daughter.

CHAPTER 27

Joe

When Audrey arrived at our makeshift camp kitchen to get in line for dinner, one of the dads in another crew made a big production of patting his pants pocket and then reaching in and pulling out his keys. "Whew!" he said. "I've still got 'em."

A few people near him chuckled. He was quite the jokester, making exaggerated claims of short-lived careers he'd had over the years, such as working in Hollywood and assigned to apply sunscreen to models at Vin Diesel's pool parties. His wife pointed out he'd never been to the West Coast. I didn't get why people laughed at his statement about car keys, but I assumed it was a reference to an earlier joke I'd missed.

At earlier meals, Audrey sat with the parents of either Colton's or Royce's crews. This time, she took her plate to one of our camp chairs outside our tent to sit alone. I looked around for her kids. The boys ate with their crews, and Simone sat with Lina and her daughter. I joined Audrey.

"Not feeling sociable tonight?" I asked.

"They know," she said.

"Know what?"

"They know I'm going to jail for stealing a car."

"How did that come out?"

"Simone couldn't keep her mouth shut."

The joke about the car keys suddenly made sense. The punchline that the man still had his keys meant they hadn't been stolen. The fact that people laughed meant the news had spread around camp. Audrey and I had agreed not to tell the Boys in Action group about her likely incarceration. If anyone commented on why she stopped coming to the weekly meetings or the next campout, we planned to say she was out of town. If they further questioned it, we would say she was taking care of a legal matter. Anything more was none of their business.

Audrey asked, "Do you remember that stoner kid back in high school who disappeared for a few months?"

"Vaguely," I said. "Was he the one named after a Star Wars character?"

"Yeah. Anakin. He lived on my block. He just stopped showing up to school."

Pieces of the story came back to me. "Didn't his parents send him to a boarding school?"

"That was the rumor," she said. "When he came back, he said he'd been staying with his grandparents. That was a load of crap. I found out a couple of years later that he was in drug rehab for those missing months. His family was able to keep it a secret the whole time."

I tried to lighten the mood. "They didn't have someone like Simone in the family."

She gave a quick snort. "No, they didn't."

A pickup truck drove past the campsite with two younger teen girls sitting on the open tailgate with a dog. They weren't part of the BIA group, but I recognized them from the park.

"Did your family do much camping?" I asked.

"We had an RV for a couple of years in middle school, but we never did tent camping."

"I thought your dad was a real outdoorsy guy."

"Not counting the sports, not really," she said. "I mean, we had the boat. And Dad and Liam hunted and fished with uncles and cousins. But that's about it. They bought the lake house after they sold the RV. Most of our vacations or weekend getaways were at the lake."

"So, no tent camping?"

"This is my first. It's not as bad as I expected. I just don't like having to walk a quarter of a mile to use the toilet."

"When I was little," I said, "most of our vacations were camping. State parks, national parks. I thought that was normal."

An extra burst of boys' laughter drew my attention back to the larger group.

"Looks like Mark's heading this way," I noted.

A bush obstructed her view of Royce's oncoming crew chief. "I don't want to talk to him," she said, ducking inside the tent before Mark noticed her.

He approached me and asked in a low voice, "What's the story I'm hearing about Royce's mother going to jail?"

CHAPTER 28

Audrey

Joe intercepted me and the kids as we came back from the showers. I'd taken Colton and Simone with me to the women's side while Royce – now officially "old enough" – handled himself in the men's. The younger two don't use the shower at home, and they treat bar soap like it's an alien artifact. They're strictly liquid-soap people. The one time I asked Joe to help with bath time, he looked at me like I'd just spoken fluent Swahili. I told him never mind.

"Come see something," he said, all mysterious. I couldn't tell if he'd discovered buried treasure or a dead body.

He led us away from our campsite, away from the glow of lanterns and s'mores-related chaos, until we stood in an empty campsite at the edge of the woods.

"What are we doing?" I asked, already imagining a pack of marshmallow-stealing raccoons plotting our demise.

Joe switched off his flashlight and whispered, "Watch."

Tiny lights flickered in the trees.

"Is someone out there?" Colton asked, because of course he assumed it was serial killers.

Joe put a calming hand on his shoulder. "It's not people."

"Fireflies," I whispered, suddenly five years old again.

Still holding Simone's hand, I set my shower tote on a picnic table and rested my free hand on Joe's shoulder.

"I haven't seen fireflies in years," I said. "The last time was with you."

"At my grandparents' place," he said. Somewhere deep in the East Texas Piney Woods, where the mosquitoes are large enough to file taxes.

He slipped the arm holding the flashlight around my waist, just like he used to, like muscle memory had kicked in.

"That was what?" he asked. "Ten years ago?"

I leaned my head against his shoulder. "Your grandfather had that theory about fireflies," I reminded him.

"They're souls waiting to be born. He totally made that up."

"Maybe he's partly right."

He snorted. "That humans start as insects?"

"No." I squeezed his shoulder. "That souls float around waiting to be born. I imagine an angel pointing at one and saying, 'Get ready, your body's almost done.' And then—whoosh—the soul zooms down like lightning and gets sucked into the new baby."

"That's better than my grandpa's story. What about the fireflies?"

"The souls hang out in fireflies for fun while they wait. They give the fireflies their light."

I leaned into him a little too enthusiastically, and he had to shift his footing to keep us both upright. The flashlight slipped from his hand, hit the gravel, and turned on. The beam washed out the fireflies completely.

I sighed. Moment over.

Royce, unimpressed, said, "They're just bugs. Can we go back now?"

The other parents weren't close enough to hear if I smacked him.

CHAPTER 29

Joe

The campsite quieted down as families settled into their tents. Kids' conversations were less with each other and more with their parents. Most kids fell asleep quickly after the active day, and a few adults came back to the campfire, monitoring its transition from flames to embers. Audrey and I carried our camp chairs over to join them.

Comfortably seated side-by-side, she tapped my forearm. "I heard you speaking Spanish with Lina today. When did you get so good at it?"

"In college. I took a semester in Spain. Stayed with a host family."

"You went to Europe?"

"Yeah." I refrained from adding that I didn't have to break up with anyone to do it. "I didn't do much touring, though. Just around Spain. And a couple of days in Paris and London on the way back."

"And now you're fluent," she said. It was a statement, not a question.

"I can understand most things, but I'm still learning business terms. I've got some clients in Puerto Rico, and I try to speak to them in Spanish when I can. But we always end up switching to English. That's where Lina's from, by the way: Puerto Rico."

"She's pretty," Audrey said.

Commenting on women's looks to other women is dangerous. The safest answer was, "I guess so." It acknowledged her comment without adding my own opinion. If I said I didn't notice, she probably wouldn't believe me, and I would be lying.

The other adults said their goodnights and went to their tents. One of the last men to leave said, "Make sure the fire's out before you go." He pointed to a bucket near the chair where he'd been sitting and said, "We saved the dirty dishwater in that bucket. Use it on the fire." Then he walked off into the shadows.

I tried to steer the conversation with Audrey back to Europe. "When you traveled in Europe, did you go to Spain?"

"Yeah." She paused, then said, "I think that's where things really went off the rails."

"What do you mean?"

"I think that's where Royce was conceived."

"But you don't remember which guy it was?"

Her arms had been on the armrests of the chair, but she suddenly pulled them in, crossed them, and looked away.

CHAPTER 30

Audrey

It felt exactly like the time my brother slapped my sunburned back "as a joke." Spoiler: I did not laugh.

Joe winced. "I didn't mean to sound judgmental." He reached over and put a hand on my forearm. "I'm just trying to get to know you again – to find out what happened in those lost years."

Why didn't you ask two months ago, genius? But sure, now is fine. Now that we're knee-deep in my European Shame Tour.

"But you know Colton's dad, right?" he asked.

I debated whether to believe he genuinely wanted to understand me or whether he was just poking around like a man inspecting a suspicious noise in the attic. But he *had* put his arm around me during the firefly moment, so I decided to give him the benefit of the doubt.

"Yeah. Eddie worked for my father," I said.

I uncrossed my arms and let my fingers trace slow circles on the back of his hand – part explanation, part distraction, part *please don't ask anything dumber.*

"Well, we called him Eddie at work," I said. "His family called him Beto. He spoke Spanish with them. But I never picked it up."

Joe probably thought I'd changed the subject, but I was actually circling back to Spain like a very messy, very emotional GPS.

"And he never taught it to Colton?" Joe asked.

"He disappeared before Colton was born."

"Disappeared? What do you mean?"

I considered stopping the hand-circles, but honestly, they were keeping *me* calm, so I kept going. "After Dad fired him, he did odd jobs around Houston. Then he found an oil field job in North Dakota – three weeks on, three weeks off. He came back a few times, then he didn't. I called his work, and they said they'd never heard of him. But he'd been sending money home, so he must've been working somewhere."

"What about his family?"

"I went by their house, and it was empty."

"What do you think happened?"

"Maybe deported," I said. "Or maybe they were afraid of being deported, so they left."

"So, they were here illegally?"

"I didn't know at the time. I found out after they disappeared. Or rather, Mom did. She went full FBI on the internet and found a reference to an Eduardo Guzman from Odessa who died as a child. Mom thinks Eddie's real name was Beto or Roberto, and he took the identity of the dead kid. Then took another identity for the North Dakota job. Apparently, there's a whole market for identities stolen from dead people. Mom tried to find the other guys Dad fired, and they also vanished."

"Why didn't Eddie – or Beto – tell you he was leaving?"

"What if my dad was the one who reported them?" I said. "He was furious at me for fooling around with the guys at the shop. That's why he fired us. And he was *super* mad at Eddie for taking me in. Dad expected me to beg him to let me come home. But I wouldn't beg. So, I went to live with Eddie. I wouldn't blame his family for not trusting me because of Dad."

Joe's questions stirred up memories I'd rather leave buried under six feet of emotional concrete. Dad wasn't just mad – he went full volcanic eruption. Right there in the repair shop waiting room. In front of customers. Called me names I wouldn't repeat to my daughter even if she burned down the house.

Joe asked, "What kind of man was this Eddie Beto, who would abandon his own kid? Even if he assumed a new identity or was forced to return to wherever he came from, why not ask his girlfriend, the mother of his child, to go with him? Not saying that's the best outcome, but if it were me, I would ask."

All I could say was, "That whole situation was messed up."

I moved my hand off of his, and he pulled his arm back to his lap. We both stared at the dim orange glow of the dying campfire. After what seemed like minutes, I said, "You're judging me, aren't you?"

"There's just so much I don't know about you," he said.

Once again, I thought, Why didn't you ask two months ago? It's not like we don't see each other every day.

He asked, "Why didn't you go back to your parents after Eddie disappeared? Surely your dad would have cooled off by then."

"I couldn't let him win."

He stared at me like I'd just insisted the sky was made of cheese.

I added, "The only reason I even got with the guys at his shop was because I knew he wouldn't like it."

"I've heard of pity sex and revenge sex," he said, "but I'm not familiar with spite sex."

If he only knew how many sub-genres my twenties contained. I was grateful he didn't ask about Simone's father. I *could* track that man down, but why? He only wanted me because he had a fetish for pregnant women. He bailed a few months after I gave birth. Joke's on him – if he'd stuck around, he could've fed that fetish for another nine months.

Joe dumped the dishwater onto the last glowing embers, and we carried our chairs back toward the tent. The camp was quiet, the kind of quiet where you can hear distant voices but not the words – just enough to feel like you're eavesdropping on ghosts. Crickets and frogs filled in the rest of the soundtrack.

Joe pulled back the flap to his side of the divided tent, but before he could disappear, I touched his arm and whispered, "Thank you for sticking up for me."

"Sure, but what do you mean?"

"I heard you talking to Mark after dinner."

"Oh, that. It's not like you stole a car to sell on the black market. You were escaping that prick Dimitri using the only means you had. And it's not like that van was worth much. I just wanted Mark to know you're not a bad person."

He said it so casually, like he hadn't just rewritten my entire moral résumé into something fit for public consumption.

Joe's conversation with Mark had happened right outside the tent, and Mark had no idea I was inside listening. Joe told him about Dimitri's "services instead of rent" proposal, but he made it sound like I'd escaped *before* agreeing to anything. He could've told the truth, but he chose to protect me – to give me a reputation I absolutely did not earn.

I wanted to hug him right then, to wrap my arms around him and say something meaningful and heartfelt.

But he ducked into the tent, a man fleeing emotional intimacy, straight to his side of the divider.

* * *

Sunday morning, some of the families had started packing up their gear before breakfast, but all stayed for the church service. Being a church-sponsored chapter of the Boys in Action, the short service was part of the program. After breakfast, a dad from one of the other crews said a prayer of praise for the weather and the safety of the campers and a request for continued safety on the drive home. Another dad gave a fifteen-minute Bible message on having a servant heart. That was probably about as long as a bunch of boys could sit still. At least he didn't speak on the commandment, "Thou shalt not steal."

* * *

Thirty minutes into the drive, I realized I hadn't heard any squabbles from the back seat. Royce rode back with the family that hauled our camping gear for us, giving Colton and Simone more breathing room in the back seat. Joe will pick him up and collect our gear after he drops the rest of us off at home.

I twisted around to check on the kids. I couldn't see Colton, but Simone had fallen asleep with her head against the window. As if reading my mind, Joe whispered, "He's asleep, too."

I asked, "I need to tell the people in our Sunday School class, don't I?"

"They're going to hear about it anyway. Maybe from someone at the campout, or maybe one of the kids will let it slip to one of their kids."

"Yeah," I said. I took a deep breath, letting it out slowly, as if preparing to deliver a speech right then and there.

He turned his head slightly to glance at me while keeping an eye on the road. "It's better that you control the narrative than them hearing it through the grapevine. I'll help."

"Thanks," I said. His version of events was better than mine.

CHAPTER 31

Joe

The party was over, and the last of Colton's friends finally left. I didn't know he had so many. We had his Boys in Action crew, a few kids from church, a few more from school, and a few siblings of those invited. I think we had eighteen kids in all, including the ones who lived here. Plus the kids' parents, plus Audrey's mother and her boyfriend, plus my parents. I'd asked my parents out of courtesy but didn't expect them to come.

Some parents stayed the whole time, some stayed only long enough to ensure we were responsible adults. I should have taken my dad's advice and held the party at a park.

Most of the activities took place in the backyard. Audrey and her mom led the kids in party games while I cooked hot dogs on the barbecue grill. Afterward, stray napkins littered the yard while remnants of destroyed balloons lay scattered about like battlefield casualties.

The previous night, Audrey had written silly activities on slips of paper and then inserted them into the balloons. They had instructions like, "Do the chicken dance," "Skip rope," and "Sing a popular song in the voice of a chipmunk. Keep it clean." We spent the morning blowing up the balloons. No helium, just exhaled air. We meant me.

In the game, when we played music, the kids tossed a balloon around to each other. When the music stopped, the last one to touch the balloon had to pop it and then follow the instructions inside, after an adult read it to them, of course. The game was probably better suited for older kids, but they still loved it. We continued until all the balloons had met their fate.

You've never heard Benson Boone's "Beautiful Things" until you've heard it sung by a choir of chipmunks.

I'd invited Lina's kids, Ethan and Hayley, mostly to keep Royce and Simone from getting bored. Ethan was Royce's friend, not Colton's, and Hayley, though older than Simone, seemed to get along well with her. They stayed longer than most, but not as long as Noah. The only reason I remembered his name was that he was the first to arrive and the last to leave. When he arrived, his mother came in with him and greeted us adults. Then she said she needed to run an errand and would be right back. I guess "right back" is relative.

After the party ended, Colton, Royce, Ethan, and Noah sat on the floor of the living room, shooting Nerf bullets at Lego towers they'd built for target practice. Simone frowned at them for excluding her. When she got tired of watching them have all the fun, she went to the dining room to stare at the large box with the picture of a bicycle on it, Beverly's gift.

Earlier, I'd heard Simone corner Beverly, who sat at the dining table drinking iced tea with her boyfriend, Dr. Alan Lane, whom her grandkids call Dr. Alan.

"Nana, I want a bicycle, too," Simone said.

"Well, when is your birthday?" Beverly asked.

"November twenty-two," Simone stated confidently. "Before Thanksgiving." Audrey had reminded her of that only yesterday when she complained of all the planning for Colton's party.

"I guess you'll have to wait till then," Beverly said.

Clouds lifted from Simone's face, and she asked hopefully, "Really, Nana?"

"I won't disappoint you, Simone. You have to be patient."

As Audrey passed by me on her way to the kitchen after seeing off the last parent and child, other than Lina, Ethan, Hayley, and Noah, she whispered, "Why is she still here?" nodding toward Lina.

Fortunately, Lina didn't hear that. She looked at Noah and offered, "Hey buddy, can Hayley and I give you a ride home?"

"No," he said. "My mom'll be here. She's always late like this."

Lina looked at me and shrugged, as if apologizing that she couldn't take Noah off our hands.

I shrugged back to indicate there was nothing she could do.

She collected leftover plastic cups from around the living room and went to the kitchen. "Do you need help?" she asked Audrey as she dropped the discarded cups into the trash can.

My mom, who had been washing plastic forks, despite being told not to save them, answered, "Thanks, but we're almost done."

"Okay, then we're going to take off," Lina said. She looked at Audrey to say, "I have to get the kids back to their dad. Thank you for inviting them. They had a great time."

"It was so great y'all came," Audrey replied, smiling. Once Lina had turned her back, Audrey's smile turned into a frown.

When Lina passed me on the way out, she lowered her voice and said, "Good luck with Noah."

Shortly after they left, Beverly called out, "Noah, I think your mother's here."

Noah dropped the Nerf gun and went to Audrey. "Miss Audrey, thank you for inviting me. I had a lovely time." To me, he said, "The hot dogs were delicious."

I swear that kid was older than six. Dad muttered something about Eddie Haskell.

"Don't forget your goodie bag," my mother reminded, pointing to the little plastic bag of party favors: a Matchbox car, cheap sunglasses, and colored pencils.

"Thank you, Joma."

I couldn't help but chuckle at his use of Mom's new nickname, her grandma name, as she called it. Noah must have heard Colton call her that. I'd introduced my mother to Audrey's kids long ago as Ms. Joanna, but apparently Simone forgot. Simone called her "Joe Momma" to her face, prompting chuckles from Dad. Mom then offered up "Jojo" as an acceptable alternative, but that didn't stick either. Simone shortened her original term to "JoeMa," and the boys followed her lead. Audrey addressed the party invitation to "Joma and Mr. Steve," and now the name is pretty much set.

* * *

As I cleaned up stray napkins littering the backyard, I found a pile of poop on the side of the house behind the air conditioner. Too big to be from a cat, and we don't have a dog.

"Audrey, come look at this," I called from the side of the house, where I tracked down a stray party napkin.

On her arrival, I pointed at the excrement.

"Eww," she squealed. "Why did you want me to see that?"

I asked, "What do you think it's from?"

With furrowed eyebrows and wrinkled nose, she said, "I don't know. A dog?"

She still didn't get it. Unless a neighbor's dog jumped the fence, did its business, and then jumped back over, I doubt it came from a dog.

I cleared my throat. "Let me ask in a different way. *Who* do you think that's from?"

As realization hit, she cried, "Eww! That's so disgusting!"

We're definitely going to have the next party at a park.

CHAPTER 32

Audrey

Mom gave Colton a bicycle – still in the box, of course, because nothing says *Happy Birthday* like assembly required. He begged to open it while the other kids were still here, but I talked him out of it.

"Are you going to ignore your friends while you try to figure out how to put it together?"

He didn't miss a beat. "Nana and Dr. Alan can put it together."

I tried logic. Rookie mistake. "If they knew how to put it together, they would've done it before bringing it over."

"Joe probably knows how to do it."

"How do you know?"

"'Cause he has tools."

I considered explaining that owning tools doesn't automatically make you Bob the Builder, but that level of nuance was going to fly straight over his head. Instead, I asked, "Are you going to let everyone take a turn riding it?"

He scowled and stomped back to his friends. Score one for Mom.

After everyone left – including my parents and Joe's parents – Colton dragged the box into the living room like a caveman hauling a mammoth.

"Can y'all help me put it together?"

I nodded toward Joe. "He's the one with the tools, remember?"

Joe smirked. "Do you even know how to ride a bike?"

I shook my head no just as Colton proudly declared, "Yeah. I watched Royce do it."

"Maybe Joe can help you if you have trouble," I said.

He ignored me. Again. Motherhood is humbling.

Joe ripped open the box like it owed him money. "You pull out the pieces," he told Colton, "while I get my toolbox."

He returned and set the toolbox on the coffee table, plopping himself down beside it. Royce hovered nearby like an apprentice in a medieval guild.

"Let's see," Joe said, flipping through the instruction manual. "We'll need an Allen wrench." He picked up a set of L-shaped tools and handed them to Colton.

"From Nana's boyfriend?" Colton asked, confused why Dr. Alan would leave his belongings here.

"Nope," Joe said. "That's just the name of the tool. Allen wrench."

I'd seen those little things my whole life and only now learned they had a name. Motherhood: where you learn alongside your children.

Royce took it from Colton. "What's it for?"

Joe waved the manual. "We'll get to that."

Then he pulled out another tool. "And we'll need pliers." He handed them to Colton.

"And…" Joe paused dramatically, "a wrench." He held it up as a prized possession. "The instructions call for a nine-sixteenths wrench, but we'll use this adjustable one. See? It has a little wheel that makes the opening bigger or smaller."

I started hauling Colton's gift pile to his room, lingering between loads to watch the bike-building saga unfold. Joe didn't just assemble the bike – he turned it into a hands-on workshop.

"That piece," Joe said, pointing, "goes there." He tapped a section of the frame. "See that hexagon hole? Find the Allen wrench that fits and turn it."

"Hegason?" Colton asked. Close enough.

"A hexagon has six sides," Royce explained, sounding like a tiny geometry professor.

Finished with the gift relocation, I plopped onto the sofa, elbows on knees, chin on clasped hands, watching them. I couldn't help smiling. Is this what a real family feels like? Dad helping his kids. Laughing. Teasing. Teaching. Mom watching proudly. Mom and Dad sleeping in separate bedrooms because one despises the other. You know – normal.

Despite Colton's confidence, after several dramatic crashes and wobbles, Joe spent the early evening jogging down the street beside him, holding the bike upright like a very patient personal trainer.

Joe shot me a dirty look when I called out, "You're getting your exercise!"

Totally worth it.

CHAPTER 33

Joe

For several nights before Audrey's sentencing hearing, I was awakened in the middle of the night by a flush, followed by the sound of bare feet on the floor. Either I've been a better sleeper before that week, or Audrey didn't usually wander around the house in the middle of the night. The night before the court hearing, I awakened to see an Audrey-sized dark shape in the doorway. Had she looked in on me on other nights and I hadn't noticed?

"Audrey?"

She took that as an invitation to enter. The shadowy mass became more distinct in the dim glow of my LED clock as she approached the bed.

"Can't sleep?" I asked unnecessarily.

"No."

I sat up in bed and grabbed my phone from the nightstand to turn on its flashlight. I should get a lamp for this side of the bed, the side closer to the bathroom, but I haven't had a pressing need for it, as I do any reading at my desk on the other side. As Audrey approached the bed, the light was enough to see that she wore her favorite oversized T-shirt that was once red but had faded to pink over the years. It covered a good portion of the black boxer shorts that I'm pretty sure she borrowed from my underwear drawer. Or maybe she just confiscated them after doing my laundry. She'd worn them as pajama bottoms for weeks. I left the phone on the nightstand, with its light shining up at the ceiling.

She pulled back the covers from the empty side of the bed and climbed in. Rather than leaning against the headboard as I did, she leaned forward and pulled her knees up to her chest, clasping her hands around them. A few weeks ago, I wouldn't have invited her into my bed. But a few weeks ago, she wasn't facing imminent jail time. I don't think she was here for a romantic interlude.

"Scared?" I asked.

"Yes."

I pulled the blanket up to cover her feet. As I reached for it, the lavender scent of her shampoo reached my nostrils, a more feminine fragrance than that of my anti-dandruff shampoo.

"I've seen the videos of ex-cons talking about prison life," she said. "I also got a taste of it myself when I was waiting for bail. Half the women there had anger issues, ready to slap anyone for just looking at them wrong. Druggies, hookers, fighters. That's what I'm going into."

I tried to console her with lame optimism. "Maybe there's still a chance the judge will show mercy and give you community service instead of approving the plea deal."

I don't know why I said that. Audrey included me on the call with her lawyer that afternoon. I specifically asked about the potential of the judge reducing her sentence, and the lawyer unequivocally told me it wouldn't happen. The hearing was merely a formality for the judge to approve the plea. They would take her into custody immediately. Thirty days minus two days for the time in the Harris County jail while she awaited bail. I thought they should have given her three days' credit for that, but the lawyer dismissed that idea, too.

"Stop it," Audrey said. "You know that's not gonna happen."

Then she surprised me with, "I deserve it."

"No, you don't. I don't care what arrangement you had with Dimitri. He took advantage of a desperate mother, and you shouldn't be the one punished."

"Yes, I should. I deserve longer. I ruined your life twice. Once, when I broke up with you, and again when I called you from jail. I ruined my father's life, which ruined my mother's life. I ruined my kids' lives by bringing them into my screwed-up world. I'm even going to mess up your mother's life."

"She volunteered," I pointed out. She offered to come to the house every weekday during Audrey's incarceration to take care of Simone, and I took her up on it. Audrey's mother agreed to come in the afternoons after her part-time job to relieve my mom and welcome the boys home from school.

"And I don't think you ruined your father's life," I told her. "He went bankrupt. Businesses fail for reasons beyond the owner's control."

"You don't get it," she said. "He fired his mechanics because of me. Then he lost customers because he couldn't hire new mechanics fast enough. He never recovered from it. He sold the boat and the lake house to keep the business going, but it wasn't enough. That's why Liam hates me. He even blames Dad's heart attack on me."

"That's going a little too far. You didn't cause his health problem."

"Mom says *she* caused his heart attack because she went to work for his rival. Dad was livid, felt like she betrayed him. But she understood the industry, and they were hiring, and Mom and Dad needed the money. But it still comes back to me."

I put my hand on her back and rubbed it gently.

"I hated Dad for what he did," she continued. "It all started with his insane plan to split us up. And I was weak and stubborn at the same time and fell for it."

I recalled her mother's reference to playing chicken.

"But I loved him, too. He was still my dad," she said. "I always thought our whole mess was temporary, and eventually I'd get my act together, and we'd all make up. I imagined spending Thanksgiving and Christmas together and Dad someday taking the kids fishing. Then he died. There was no going back. The house was still there. Mom was still there. But without Dad, the picture I had in my head broke into little pieces."

I didn't agree with her assessment of causing his demise. "He's the one who basically screwed up everything for you."

"I should have learned my lesson before," she said. "I leave, things happen, I can never go back."

"Learned your lesson? Something else happened with your dad?"

"With you."

"What do you mean?"

"When we broke up, I didn't think it would be permanent. I thought we could get back together after the Europe trip."

That was doubtful. The breakup felt rather permanent at the time. I went off to college, eventually got over her, and moved on. "Even if I'd waited around for you, your dad would have started all over again with his insults and condescension."

Besides playing golf, I also ran cross-country track. Her dad claimed that playing football like he and Audrey's brother did taught men to head into a fight. Track only taught me to run away. In other words, a cowardly sport. On another occasion, I was at her house as her mother carried in groceries from the car. A package of Maxipads fell out of a bag, and her dad picked them up and tossed them to me, saying, "She got you something." As with most of his insults, Audrey just groaned, "Daaaad!"

"You were the only boyfriend who wasn't intimidated by him," she said. "Oliver, back in ninth grade, never made it past the first date. At least Toby lasted a couple of months."

"Not intimidated? He intimidated the hell out of me. Nothing I did was good enough. Remember when we went to the lake? I swear he was trying to drown me. Don't you remember when he swerved the boat on purpose and made me fall in? Twice!"

"It was all for show. And you always kept your cool."

Isn't that how you deal with bullies, don't give them the satisfaction of letting them know it bothers you, even if it does? A lot of good that did, though.

You dumped me and hooked up with random European dudes, I thought. But this was one of those times when I wasn't supposed to offer a solution or counter her points. My role was merely to listen.

"I tried to call you," is said, "but you were already gone."

"I know. I got your message. But you were about to leave for college, and I realized it was foolish to think we could get back together." She gave a heavy sigh. "I couldn't face talking to you. I basically cheated."

Did she mean deceiving me by pretending everything was fine while planning the breakup?

"I still loved you," she said. "But by that time, I'd already done things I shouldn't have. I cheated on you. You deserved better."

She lowered her voice into an almost imperceptible whisper. "I lost everything. You. My friends. My dad. My reputation. And now my freedom. And in between, I got babies I wasn't prepared for. And who's gonna hire an ex-con?"

There's something about a woman's vulnerability that puts me into protective mode. I put my arm around her and pulled her close. She unclasped her hands and let her knees fall toward me as she rested her head on my shoulder. After several minutes of silence, she slid out of my embrace and curled up next to me, her hands under the pillow.

I adjusted the covers over us both and then whispered, "Good night, Audrey."

She answered with slow, steady breaths.

CHAPTER 34

Audrey

The kids knew I was leaving, but I tried to act like it was a regular school day. Totally normal. Nothing to see here. Except we said our goodbyes *inside* the house, and then I stayed hidden while Joe and his mom walked the boys to the bus stop, pretending that everything was fine. I didn't want the boys to witness me melting into a puddle. Unfortunately, I didn't have a similar escape plan for Simone, so she got front-row seats to the emotional breakdown. When Joe and his mother came back, they found us on the sofa – Simone on my lap, both of us bawling like we'd just watched the end of *Toy Story 3*.

By the time we had to leave for the courthouse in Beaumont, I'd finally pulled myself together. For the solemn occasion, I wore a white turtleneck to hide my tattoos and a navy blazer to hide my personality. I'd taken out my piercings the night before, and now my cheeks had tiny dents where the dimple piercings used to be. Very professional. Very "I definitely don't steal vans."

What was I pretending to be? A banker? An accountant? A soccer mom? No—soccer moms at our church wear dresses and have hair that never frizzes. Everyone in the courtroom would see right through me. The whole situation was just so... *Copenhagen.*

Joe came in and stood behind me, looking at me through the mirror. "You look nice."

"Not like a car thief, right?" I asked, fishing for reassurance.

He put his hands on my shoulders. "No. Just ... pretty."

No one had called me pretty in years. I didn't think it mattered until my eyes started misting up again.

I croaked out, "Thank you."

He kissed my right cheek – right on the little crater left by my piercing – and said, "We need to go. Don't want to make the judge angry."

Joe took the day off work to drive me. His mother handed me a box of tissues. We made it to the courthouse with thirty minutes to spare, and I had managed to stop crying by the time we passed Baytown. But not before he grabbed a tissue and dabbed the corner of his eyes. When we parked, my tears started flowing again.

"Get it all out now," Joe said. "Remember…."

"No crying in jail," I finished. We'd watched enough YouTube ex-con videos to know the rules.

He reached across the console and took my hand. We didn't speak; we just sat together in silence for probably twenty minutes. And then, still without words, he let go of my hand, and we both opened our doors.

CHAPTER 35

Joe

Seeing her in the outfit she picked for court, Audrey reminded me of the sweet, innocent girl I knew in high school. No piercings. No visible tattoos. Maybe her vulnerability in this situation added to the image. How could the judge not have mercy on her and reduce her sentence to probation?

But there was no courtroom miracle. The judge read the plea deal and asked Audrey if she accepted it. When she confirmed her acceptance, the judge announced that her sentence started today, confirming what the lawyer had told us. Then he granted her permission to say final goodbyes to her loved ones. I guess that was me. I had offered to bring her mother with us, but Audrey didn't want her there. She said her mother would cause a scene and make her more upset.

That was it. A short and simple formality to start her sentence at the Haney State Women's Correctional Facility in Liberty County. Did anyone else see the irony of being imprisoned in a county called Liberty? At least it was closer to home than Beaumont.

As the two bailiffs stood by, Audrey turned to me, standing behind her at the railing that separated the spectator gallery from the legal proceedings. She had almost no emotion on her face. Then she took a deep breath and turned around to lean back against the railing, against me. I reached over and wrapped my arms around her, squeezing her tight.

"We'll come every weekend to see you," I assured. "And I'll put money in your commissary account as soon as they have you set up in the system."

"Thank you for being here, Joe."

I released her when one of the bailiffs approached to lead her out a side door.

By the time I got home, Audrey's mom had already arrived to start her shift with the kids. I nodded to her to indicate it was done. With one look at me, her face twisted up, and tears began flowing. My mom handed her the box of tissues from the coffee table. Mom had always been the self-designated tissue keeper.

* * *

Thankfully, Beverly got her emotions under control by the time the boys' bus arrived. This was the first time I'd been at the bus stop to welcome them home. The bus stop moms took notice of Audrey's absence and gave me knowing looks, little nods, and half smiles.

The one mom who hadn't been at the bus stop that morning said, "This was the day, wasn't it, Joe?"

They all knew what "the day" referred to. Who didn't know about Audrey's situation? The kids didn't understand the need to keep certain things private. I introduced the moms to Beverly and explained she would be meeting the boys at the bus stop in the afternoons. Most had met my mother that morning.

The mom dressed in medical scrubs introduced herself to Beverly. "I'm Amber, Katy's mom," she said, as if Beverly knew who Katy was. Then she pointed to her house, "I live in that house with the blue door. If you need anything, just ask."

She then placed her hand on my arm. "That goes for you, too, Joe. I know what it's like to raise kids alone. Things were quite a struggle after my divorce."

"Well, Beverly's here for the afternoons," I reminded.

Gazing intently into my eyes, she said, "I'm sure she can't be here twenty-four hours a day." She squeezed my arm and added, "I'll check up on you." Then she winked.

I forced a smile and responded with a polite, "Thanks."

Once her daughter exited the bus, she turned and waved at me before following her daughter to the house with the blue door.

Before the boys walked up, and as Simone played with a small dog brought by one of the mothers, Beverly looked at me with raised eyebrows and gave a slight nod in the direction of Amber and Katy.

I sucked air through clenched teeth and replied, "Don't worry. She's probably close to forty, and I'm not into cougars."

When the boys stepped off the bus, they each had different reactions to seeing their grandmother. Colton excitedly shouted, "Nana!" and raced to her. Royce looked at me with sad eyes and said, "Momma's gone, isn't she?"

"Yeah. But you'll get to see your Nana more. Isn't that a good thing?"

He looked at me like I was stupid. "Not as good as seeing Momma."

* * *

Beverly stayed to prepare dinner and thankfully oversee the kids' bathtime. Royce just turned eight and could take care of himself in the bathroom, but I wasn't sure I was ready to deal with a four and a six-year-old in the tub. I had no idea what Audrey did with them in the bathroom. Did she scrub them down or merely supervise while they washed themselves? They may have lived with me for the past few months, but they weren't related to me, and just thinking through the logistics of the process probably violated some law.

Beverly left right after that. I was proud of myself for getting them to bed at their usual times. I hadn't been involved in tucking the kids in bed until about a week before, when Audrey rightly thought the kids needed to get used to me. I tucked them into their beds, and all of us felt the absence of their mother. Things felt off, but at least we maintained the proper schedule.

Until Simone came creeping into my bedroom as I brushed my teeth.

"Where's Mommy?"

"You're supposed to be asleep," I pointed out with a mouthful of toothpaste.

"Where's Mommy?"

I spat and said, "You know where Mommy is. She has to be away for a while."

She whined, "I want Mommy."

I carried her back to her room, tucked her into bed, and stayed with her until she fell asleep. Then I went to bed myself.

I was back in court. This time, I was the defendant. I don't even know what the crime was, only that the judge just proclaimed my sentence. I looked around the gallery at the spectators. Griffin, Audrey, her parents, my parents, and Dimitri, the tow truck driver. Audrey stepped forward, saying, "I'm sorry, Joe." Then the bailiff patted my shoulder to get my attention.

Simone patted my shoulder, saying, "Joe, wake up."

I groggily opened my eyes, thankful I wasn't in court. I checked the clock. One thirty.

She whined, "I want to sleep with you."

I briefly considered her request as it required little effort to pull her up onto the bed and go back to sleep. But I then decided it would set a bad precedent, not to mention what people might think if word got out that I shared a bed with an unrelated little girl. I carried her back to her room and repeated the process from earlier.

"You're not doing it right," she whined.

"What do you mean?"

"You didn't tuckle me in right," she said.

Tuckle? I reflected on the process. Get her in bed; say the prayer, a step Audrey added when we started going to church; turn off the light; say good night, and leave.

"We said the prayer the first time," I reminded her, assuming that was the part I didn't get right with the second and this third attempt. "I didn't think we needed to say it again."

"No," she said, indicating the lack of prayer wasn't the cause of not getting the tuckle right. "You're 'posed to say 'I love you'. Mommy always says 'I love you' 'fore she turns off the light. And then I say it back."

We didn't cover this in Debbie's parenting class. Besides, I wasn't Simone's parent.

To stall while I processed this, I asked, "Are those the rules?"

She nodded. "Umm hmm."

Am I allowed to tell someone else's kids I love them? More importantly, *do* I love them? What does that even mean? I finally determined that at only the tender age of four, she couldn't possibly understand all the implications of loving someone.

"Then I guess I'd better do it," I said. I cleared my throat and said, "Simone, I love you."

"I love you, too."

In my head, I added, *Now go to sleep.*

In the morning, when I went to get the boys up for school, I found her in the lower bunk with Colton. That night, I set up a cot for her in the boys' room, on condition that on Sunday night, she would go back to her own bed. I wanted to keep further disruptions of school night routines to a minimum.

* * *

Friday night, when Beverly left for the evening, I knew the weekend was my responsibility. I wouldn't have Beverly or Mom to keep the kids occupied or entertained. At shower time every night, I noticed

Audrey's towel hanging on the rod. I should have moved it to her laundry basket days ago, but I hadn't. Each night, I left it hanging next to mine.

Saturday, after sweating in the sun from mowing the lawn, I went for my usual shower. The towels still hung on the rod, hers and mine side-by-side, waiting to be used. On other Saturdays, I had to grab a fresh towel from the cabinet as Audrey would have taken the old ones to wash. I'd forgotten that laundry was another task I had to manage myself. I reached for her towel to toss into her basket but stopped myself. It could hang there for a few more minutes until I was done.

That evening, after a dinner of one of Audrey's specialties, Spam cubes, scrambled eggs, and hashbrowns, I found a child-appropriate movie to stream on the TV for the kids and sat at the coffee table to fold the freshly washed laundry: mine, the kids', and Audrey's. In all my years of bachelorhood, I'd never done laundry for others. The kids' clothes were something of a curiosity, undies with pictures of cartoon characters and miniature versions of shirts and pants.

Mom and Beverly had taken care of meals for the last few days, with Beverly even overseeing the kids' baths before I came home. But folding their clothes that evening drove home the idea that I was their caregiver. I finished folding their clothes, placing them in three separate stacks on the sofa, and moved on to the adult clothes. The next article I picked up was a pair of Audrey's panties. For reasons I cannot explain, I sort of felt dirty for handling something so intimate. I quickly folded it and started a new stack.

When the movie ended, Royce got up off the floor and announced, "I'm taking a bath first."

That prompted Simone to look at me and ask, "Since Nana's not here, are you doing my bath tonight?"

Colton sneered. "Men don't give girls baths."

Royce corrected him. "Momma told him what to do. I heard her."

Colton said, "Well, I can do my bath myself."

My response was, "Good for you!"

Simone just looked at me with big eyes, expecting an answer from me as if she hadn't heard her brothers.

I asked, "You can't do it yourself?"

Royce looked at me like I was stupid. "She'll slip and fall and break her head. Then she'll bleed everywhere, and you'll have to take her to the hospital."

She shook her head. "You're 'posed to help me and give me the towel when I'm done."

"Can I do it with my eyes closed?" I asked.

She tilted her head slightly. "Then you won't see me."

That's the point, I thought.

CHAPTER 36

Audrey

Haney State only allows visitors on Saturdays and Sundays, and they have to sign up in advance, like it's a brunch reservation instead of jail. But no one would tell me if anyone had actually signed up for me. Every time I asked, the staff gave me the same line: "We'll let you know when the time comes." They said it with the enthusiasm of DMV employees who've achieved inner peace through apathy. Honestly, I think they take pride in being unhelpful. It's their sport.

Saturday visitation came and went with no notice. When I asked again, they blinked at me like confused owls. "We'll let you know." Sure you will, Brenda.

I discovered that if I cried in the shower *quietly*, no one could tell. The water masked everything. And if a sob slipped out, I could cover it with a couple of coughs. "Sorry," I'd say. "I yawned and got water in my throat." Totally believable. Happens to everyone. Nothing to see here.

Saturday night, I dreamed I was back on the lake in my dad's ski boat with Dad, Liam, and Joe. Classic family outing: sunshine, water, and my father driving like he was auditioning for *Fast & Furious: Midlife Crisis Edition.*

Dad swerved hard, and Joe flew into the water while Dad and Liam laughed like hyenas. Then Dad swerved the other way, and *I* went flying in. The boat sped off, leaving Joe and me bobbing in the lake like two abandoned pool noodles.

A sleek speedboat pulled up next to Joe and the boaters hauled him in like he was a celebrity rescue mission. I yelled, "Joe! Joe!" trying to get his attention, but they pointed the boat toward the shore and zoomed off, leaving me behind, the unwanted extra in my own dream.

Apparently, I yelled loud enough in real life to wake the dead, because one of my bunkmates shouted, "Shut up!"

In the morning, another one asked, "Who's Joe? Boyfriend?"

"Sort of," I said.

She snorted. "Honey, if you don't know, then he's not."

Then she went straight for the follow-up. "How long you in for?"

I'd told her before, but jail time apparently resets people's memory. "Twenty-five more days."

She shrugged. "Maybe he wait for you; maybe not. Longer'n that, he gonna be off with some other shawty."

Comforting. Truly.

Around two o'clock, a guard came to get me. "You got visitors."

Finally – something that didn't involve dreams, drowning, or unsolicited relationship advice from women who snore like chainsaws.

* * *

When I saw my kids, it felt like stumbling onto an oasis after wandering the desert for days – except instead of water, I got three small humans launching themselves at me while yelling "Momma!" and "Mommy!" loud enough to make the entire visitation room turn and stare. Parents smiled knowingly. Child-free visitors looked like they regretted every life choice that brought them here.

The visitation room wasn't like in the movies – no glass wall, no scratchy phone handset from 1972. Just tables, chairs, and the faint smell of disinfectant. They even let Simone and Colton sit in my lap. Royce probably could've, too, but he's reached that age where physical affection must be rationed like wartime sugar. He hugged me, then slid into the seat next to Joe.

After the kids and I exchanged a flurry of "I missed you," Joe said, "I missed you, too."

"You probably miss my cooking and doing your laundry," I said, trying to sound tough and failing spectacularly.

He blinked at me, and that was all it took. Toughness: gone. I wiped my eyes with my bare hand, then wiped my hand on my shirt like a classy lady and reached across the table to grab his hand.

"Thank you for bringing them," I croaked. "Even if Mom had been willing to bring the kids, I'm glad you came."

"You look good," he said. "Are you okay?"

I nodded. Jail was… not great. I was always sweaty, everyone was rude, and the food tasted like sadness. Stale sadness. But the YouTube ex-cons warned me not to complain out loud. Apparently jail has Yelp reviewers with fists.

Royce studied my outfit. "I thought prisoners wore orange."

"Not at this jail," I said. "Everyone wears white. White pants, white shirt, white shoes."

I still don't know why. Maybe they want us to look like rejected boy-band members.

Joe said, "Your mom finally got an offer on her house."

"Is she taking it?"

"Yeah. Closing's in a few weeks. I offered to help her move, but she said she'd rather hire professionals. I didn't know whether to be offended or relieved."

"Definitely relieved," I said. Moving is the devil's cardio.

"Besides," I added, "that tiny house she's getting won't fit much. She's been purging for weeks."

"Nana's moving?" Colton asked, as if this was brand-new information. Kids hear nothing unless it involves snacks.

"Yep. She'll live next door to Uncle Johnny."

Colton turned to Joe. "He has horses."

I jumped in. "Want to hear a funny story?" No one answered, but I forged ahead. "There were a couple of women riding in the van with me from the Beaumont jail. One of them looked like a soccer mom – makeup, ponytail, the whole PTA vibe."

Royce asked, "Why was she going to jail?"

"I don't know, Sweetie. We don't ask that." I leaned in, lowering my voice. "Anyway, she asked me for tips on how to survive in jail. *Me.* Can you believe it?"

Joe leaned in too, amused. "So what did you tell her?"

"I just rolled with it. Talked tough. Gave her all the advice I learned from YouTube like I'd lived it myself. Don't cry. Brush your teeth before breakfast so your morning breath doesn't get you punched. You know – practical stuff."

We talked about school, and Simone told me how she was getting along with Nana and Joma.

"Joe doesn't know anything about putting kids to bed," Colton announced.

"Yeah," Simone agreed. "We had to teach him everything."

I snickered at Joe.

"Hey, I'm doing better," he said, suddenly defensive. He looked at all three kids. "Right? I'm doing better, right?"

Royce shrugged. "You're getting there."

When the guard came over and cleared her throat, I wasn't ready. I wanted to glue myself to my kids.

"Just a few more minutes," I begged.

She curled her lip. "Don't cause a scene in front of your kids."

Colton and Simone started crying, which definitely counted as a scene, but apparently that was fine. Joe leaned across the table to peel Simone off me while the guard grabbed my elbow. I told the kids I loved them as fast as I could before being escorted away.

Right before the door closed, I called, "Joe, thank you!"

Then the door shut, and my tears came back with a vengeance. So much for taking my own advice.

CHAPTER 37

Joe

Only a few miles from the jail, I heard the police siren. I saw through the mirror the patrol car catching up to us, so I slowed and pulled to the right, hugging the shoulder and leaving plenty of room for the Sheriff's Deputy to pass. But he didn't pass. He tailgated me until I uttered one of Audrey's forbidden words – the non-Nordic version – and stopped the car.

Colton and Simone started crying while we waited for the deputy to come to the car. While I pulled out my driver's license and insurance card, Colton announced, "It's a lady police."

When she arrived at my window, I held up my license before she could ask.

She took it and asked, "Do you know why I stopped you?"

"Broken taillight?" I asked, knowing there was nothing wrong with the taillights. I didn't want to confess to speeding.

She pursed her lips slightly as if she knew I wasn't that naïve. "You were going twelve over the speed limit," she said dryly.

I don't think she had paid attention to the kids in the back seat until Colton asked, "Are you gonna take us to jail?"

Royce, from his narrow space squished between Colton and Simone, patted both of his siblings and said, "She can't take all of us to jail, 'cause we won't fit in her car. She'll only take Joe."

For some reason, that made Simone cry more.

The deputy lowered her head to get a better view of the back seat. "Not for speeding," she said.

Then she looked at me and added, "But maybe for child endangerment."

I twisted around to see the kids. All three wore their seat belts. "What do you mean?"

"The one in the middle should be in a booster seat," she said.

"Three boosters won't fit in the back," I pointed out, knowing my answer wouldn't be acceptable. "Can he sit in the front?"

She looked at Royce for two seconds, then looked at me for another second as if she thought I was an idiot. "He's too small. If you get in an accident, the airbag could kill him."

Joe said, "This is the only car I have."

She said, "Borrow one, rent one, whatever. I don't care. You need to keep these kids safe."

I drove like an angry grandpa the rest of the way home. That is, I kept a scowl on my face as I drove exactly at the speed limit. A few cars honked at us as they passed.

* * *

When I came home from work on Monday, the changes to the living room shocked me.

"What the hell's going on here!?" I shouted at Beverly.

"I knew he'd be mad," Royce said.

The walls were covered in graffiti. At least that's what it looked like to me. The sofa was pushed toward the middle of the room, and the walls were covered in drawings of stick figures, mountains, airplanes, cars, and animals I didn't recognize. Not drawn on paper attached to the walls, but drawn directly onto the walls.

"Don't blame me," Beverly said, chuckling. "Your mom started it."

"Joma brought markers," Simone said, as if that meant that marking the walls was a reasonable progression. "And she drew that tree," she said, pointing to a primitive drawing of a tree on the wall adjacent to the kitchen.

Beverly's smile faded when I didn't seem amused. "She said you're painting the rooms, so all this will get covered."

I looked around again. Before today, it might have only taken one coat of paint to cover the gray walls. With this mess, it will take two.

"I drew that car," Colton said proudly. "That yellow stuff is fire coming out the back because it's a rocket car."

Mom has been pushing me for months to paint the interior. It just hasn't been a high priority. This must be her way of forcing me to do it.

"I don't have time to paint," I complained to Beverly. "Especially now that I have to take care of the kids." Beverly and my mom help me during the week, but it's all on me in the evenings and on weekends.

Beverly pointed to the kitchen table. "She left you a note."

The note said, "We're painting everything white unless you say otherwise. Love Mom."

White? Now it will need three coats.

"Who's we?" I asked, more to myself than anyone present.

"Me and Joma," Simone answered.

I shook my head at the idea that my mom and a four-year-old would paint the house. I left my credit card next to the note to cover the paint supplies.

I thought Mom was burdened enough with just watching Simone. Now she's painting too? In all fairness, she did volunteer to come over and see the boys off at the bus stop and watch Simone. She said it would be grandma practice. Who knew grandma practice included home renovation?

I didn't notice the new photo on the mantle until after dinner. It was a framed 8x10-inch photo of me and Audrey at prom. We both look so young. Later, I found out Beverly came across the photo while packing up her house to move out. I'm sure she has more recent photos of Audrey; I don't know why she picked that one. Royce said it doesn't look like his mother. Her kids only remember her with tats and piercings.

That night, I sent a text to the BIA parents group asking if anyone had happened to get a photo of Audrey at the campout. Lina responded with a couple of candid shots. Then she called.

"Are those what you're looking for?" she asked. "I might have more, but I think she's closer to the camera in the ones I sent you than in my other ones."

"Yeah, those are good," I said. "I'm looking for something I can hang on the wall to keep her face in front of her kids while she's, uh, you know, away."

"So, just her, without other people?"

"Ideally," I said.

"Hold on," she said. I could hear her kids, the TV, or something in the background for several minutes. She broke the silence a few times with comments like, "That should just about do it," "Just a little more," and "Almost there."

She finally said, "I did a little quick editing, and now I'm sending it to Walgreens for printing."

"You don't have to do that," I said.

I detected a hint of amusement in her voice when she said, "Too late."

I hadn't wanted to pull others into our situation. I said, "I'll pay you back."

"This is my gift to her kids," she replied. "You can pay me back by bringing ice cream to my apartment on Saturday afternoon."

"Huh? Did I miss something?" I asked.

"I like French Vanilla. My kids like Cookies and Cream. Surprise us. We'll make it a playdate."

It's a good thing I didn't have other plans. "What time?"

"Two," she said. "And bring swimsuits. We can hang out by the pool, and afterward, we'll order pizza and play games."

* * *

I could tell from the architectural style that the apartment complex was old. Probably from the mid-seventies, like my neighborhood. It stood out from the other old apartment complexes with its modern updates. The brick veneer was painted light gray with dark gray trim. The window shutters were board-and-batten style, in a weathered oak stain. I learned a lot about architectural features from my realtor.

Lina answered her door, and I immediately thought, *Wow!* A few years ago, I might have said it out loud. But years of conditioning from HR harassment training made me hold back.

She wore a white two-piece swimsuit with a large black scarf wrapped around her waist and tied at her right hip. Her hair fell loosely around her shoulders, a change from the ponytail she often wore to the BIA meetings. No piercings other than her earlobes. Her one tattoo, a small heart on her left ankle. I felt overdressed in a golf shirt and shorts.

"Hey, guys!" she greeted cheerfully, opening the door wider and stepping aside to let us pass. "Ethan and Hayley have been asking all day when you're coming."

The kids spotted hers in the living room and ran inside without further invitation. They also wore their swimsuits. Lanky Ethan in orange trunks and his sister Hayley in a yellow two-piece with ruffles.

She nodded to the gym bag in my hand and said, "I hope that's your swimsuit."

"Towels," I answered. "We're wearing our swimsuits under our clothes." I didn't feel the need to tell her the bag also contained clean underwear to change into after swimming.

She cocked her head to the side with a slight smile. "Good. Then I don't have to push you into the pool with your clothes on."

Her living room looked comfortably lived in. A Hot Wheels racetrack spilled over from the coffee table to the floor with little cars scattered about. Barbie dolls protruded from a basket in the corner like a bouquet of little human flowers. The credenza under the TV held a stack of children's board games. I recognized Sorry, Trouble, Guess Who, and Twister from my childhood.

In the summer before eleventh grade. My sister Ava found Audrey and me entangled on the floor of the living room in a questionable position on the Twister mat. We'd been giving each other our own appendage and color calls rather than using the game spinner. Ava thought it was hilarious. Mom was horrified. Dad threw out the game after that.

Royce and Colton went straight for the Hot Wheels cars. Hayley grabbed Simone's hand and said, "Come see my room."

* * *

I sat on the edge of the deep end of the rectangular pool with Lina to my right, our feet in the water, monitoring the kids and sipping lemonade from plastic cups. At this pool, deep meant five feet. I hadn't even thought of Audrey's kids' swimming skills until we arrived at the pool. Fortunately, the boys could swim, and Lina let Simone borrow Hayley's old floaties. Still, I made sure she stayed in the shallow end.

"You really need to get her swim lessons," Lina said.

Another responsibility for a kid who wasn't mine. "Or maybe we just don't go near water," I said, with an exaggerated smile.

"I'm serious," she said. "It's a survival skill."

I learned at the neighborhood pool when I was about Simone's age, but I can barely remember. My neighborhood didn't have a pool, and the one in my parents' neighborhood is closed until spring. The YMCA advertised swim lessons a few months ago on the electric sign outside their building.

"Survival skill, huh?" I echoed. *And guess who would have to pay for it,* I thought. "I'll mention it to Audrey."

"How did she and her kids come to live with you?"

"I had a house, and they needed a place to stay," I said, giving the most basic answer.

"She said you two used to date in high school. So even though it didn't work out between you two back then, you stayed in touch?"

I leaned back on my elbows and looked up at the clouds. "No. I hadn't seen her in years. Didn't know she had kids. A few months ago, she called me out of the blue to meet for coffee."

"And you fell in love all over again," Lina guessed. Or was she teasing?

"Not hardly. She was a mess. Single mom, questionable lifestyle, signs of mental or emotional trauma. When I sensed she wanted more than to catch up, I bolted."

"I'm a single mom," Lina pointed out.

I tried to qualify my comment to redeem myself. "Oh, uh, sorry. But you seem to have your life together. Nice apartment, good job, no nose ring, no giant lotus on your neck. You're a lawyer, right?"

"Paralegal," she corrected.

"And I assume your ex helps."

Lina slid into the water and turned to face me, putting her crossed arms on the edge of the pool to keep herself in place. "Financially, sure. But he could do better with spending time with them. Like, taking Ethan to the campouts."

"Audrey didn't have that stability," I said. "And one coffee date wasn't going to get me involved. Someone else made the mess; someone else should clean it up." That sounded harsh. "I mean," I continued, "she dumped me right after high school. No contact for years. She was practically a stranger when she showed up at the coffee shop."

I braced myself for criticism for being callous to someone who clearly needed help, but Lina just asked, "What changed your mind?"

"A week later, when she was locked out of her mom's house – her mom was on vacation – and she had nowhere else to go, she called me in desperation, and I let her stay over."

"And then they stayed for good," she guessed.

For good? Is that what this arrangement is? Our agreement went through the school year, but does Audrey think this is permanent?

"There was a little more to it, but that's basically it." I left out the part of God messing with my head. That sounded crazy even to me.

She stretched her arms out in front of her, sliding them apart until her right arm touched my hip. "I admire you for getting involved. Any regrets?"

I watched the boys toss colorful rings into the water, then jump in and compete to retrieve them before the others. Hayley showed Simone how to float on her back.

"Well, I wasn't counting on her going to jail," I said. "I thought the case would be dropped, or at worst, she would get probation. Even before she went to jail, I missed hanging out with my friends. Now, I've got to think about other people before I do anything. I can't even watch what I want on TV. That is, if I had time to watch TV. And I definitely can't jump in the car for a last-minute weekend trip to San Antonio."

I didn't realize how much I'd been domesticated until I described it out loud.

"Did you do much of that before Audrey?" Lina asked.

I looked out to see Hayley face down in the water. "Hey! Is Hayley okay!?" I shouted.

Lina turned to look as Ethan swam to his sister and grabbed her foot. She kicked him and jerked her head up out of the water, took a deep breath, and yelled, "Stop!" Then, "Momma!"

Lina called out, "Y'all be nice to each other!" Then, to me, she said, "She's okay," and turned back to her earlier position of leaning against the edge of the pool.

As if a near-drowning never happened, she restated her earlier question. "Did you do many of those last-minute trips before Audrey and the kids moved in?"

"Not really," I admitted. "It's just that now I can't if I wanted. Maybe if I really planned it out. Another thing is that nowadays I have to pay more attention to costs."

She leaned over and bumped her shoulder against my thigh. "Now you have to act like a responsible adult."

If we'd been sitting across a table in a conference room, I'd be irritated at her lack of empathy. But in swimsuits at the pool, with her looking up at me from her position in the water, I took it as teasing rather than condescension.

"At least pretend to feel sorry for me," I said with faux indignation.

"I get it. Parenting is hard. I eased into it one at a time. You got hit with it suddenly."

I tapped her hip with my foot and said, "I did make some new friends." Odd that all of them were parents.

She raised her nearly empty cup of lemonade and said, "Here's to new friends."

I had to switch my cup to my right hand to meet her toast. Then I asked, "How did you handle things when you and your ex split up? I mean, you had two kids. Did life get harder?"

"Honestly, I was doing most of the parenting and housework before the divorce, so it didn't feel that different. The biggest change was that he's not around to help drive the kids to their activities. Gymnastics. Soccer. BIA meetings. I ended up cutting soccer. I told Hayley she'd have to give up gymnastics if she wants to join Girl Scouts."

Then she asked, "How are you managing without Audrey?"

"Our moms have been helping during the week. Fortunately, the busy season's over at work. It's still been a little rough, though. The kids have regressed a little in discipline. I thought we had tantrums under control, but Simone and Colton had a couple of meltdowns this week. And they seemed clingier for a couple of days after visiting their mother."

Lina's phone chimed, and she pointed to it. "Can you pass me that?"

She checked it and looked up toward one of the buildings that surrounded the pool and waved. Then she looked at me and asked, "Do you mind if Grant joins us?"

"Grant?"

"From BIA. Alex's dad. He lives in the complex, but Alex is with his mother this weekend."

I tried to stifle my disappointment at having to share Lina's company with another guy and said, "Sure."

She set the phone on the deck and extended her hand. "Help me out."

* * *

We didn't stay long at the pool after Grant arrived. We all went back to Lina's place and ordered pizzas. After changing out of our swimsuits, we adults sat at the table with iced tea while Colton focused on the Hot Wheels track in the living room, and the other kids disappeared into Ethan and Hayley's bedrooms. Lina still looked good, even in sweatpants and a tank top.

"Joe," Simone called as she came out of Hayley's room holding a pencil and a pad of drawing paper. "Draw us a mermaid." Then she turned to Hayley and said, "He can draw lots of stuff."

I took the pencil and pad and began sketching out the shape of a woman's top half with a fish's bottom half. I'm no Rembrandt, but I can do a fair cartoon drawing.

"Should I give her braided pig tails?" I teased Simone.

"Joe!" she said with an attitude. "Mermaids don't have pigtails. Duh!"

"Okay. No pigtails. You don't have to get so huffy about it." I drew strands of hair flowing behind her, adding tiny fish swimming among her locks.

What color is her hair?" I asked that even though I only had a plain old gray pencil.

"Red, like Ariel."

"Okay." I wrote the word "red" above the figure's head and drew an arrow pointing at the hair.

I looked at Lina and Grant and said, "I guess I should make it rated G," as I added a bikini top to the mermaid's chest.

"Not for my sake," Grant chuckled.

"I'll make one for you later," I joked. "Should I give her Lina's face?"

Lina looked from me to Grant, then back to me, with her mouth open. "Not if you're going to make her topless."

Grant and I laughed at her faux discomfort. I doubted I could draw a person accurately enough that people would know who it was. I finished the mermaid, signed my name at the bottom of the page, and then handed the pad back to Simone.

"Not bad," Lina said. "Do you draw much?"

"He draws me pictures all the time. Whatever I ask for," Simone said.

Lina raised her eyebrows like she was impressed. "Like what?" she asked.

"Mostly ponies and princesses," Simone answered. "He draws spaceships and trucks and stuff for Colton."

"You left out the flying shark," I said.

Simone scrunched up her face. "Nobody asked for that. You just drew it for yourself."

After the pizza, the kids played Candy Land, and we adults played Jinga.

As much as I didn't want to leave Grant and Lina alone together, even though her kids were there, at the first yawn from Colton, which spread to Simone, I announced that I needed to get the kids home and ready for bed. It was only eight thirty.

As I gathered my gym bag and damp towels, Lina said, "I almost forgot." She quickly went to the TV credenza, grabbed a two-foot-long cardboard tube that I hadn't previously noticed, and presented it to me.

"What's this?"

"The picture of Audrey. My gift to the kids."

The tube contained a 24-inch by 36-inch life-size poster of Audrey's torso and smiling face, looking slightly to the side at something out of the camera frame.

"I took that shot when we were at the playground," Lina said.

We exchanged hugs, and I looked back at Grant, sitting on the sofa with no sign of leaving. He saluted. "See you Tuesday."

CHAPTER 38

Audrey

I guess Joe is sticking with the Sunday afternoon visitation schedule. Personally, I'd prefer Saturdays so I could spread out my *extracurricular activities* – you know, crying, panicking, and staring at the ceiling—but beggars can't be choosers. At least I got visitors two weeks in a row. Some inmates haven't seen anyone in months. Meanwhile, I'm over here getting weekly letters complete with photos and a recap of the kids' days. Joe calls it his "dinner discussion digest," like he's running a tiny newsroom.

I kissed all my kids the second they were within reach. Royce looked around the visitation room, checking for paparazzi before reluctantly letting me kiss him. Joe chuckled. Royce just turned eight and already acts like he's too cool for maternal affection. At this rate, he'll be rolling his eyes in full sentences by age nine.

I smiled at Joe, and he leaned in for a hug. I teased, "Do you want a kiss, too?"

He chuckled. "A hug is fine."

Naturally, I kissed him on the cheek anyway before he could escape.

I pulled Colton and Simone onto my lap like last week and commanded, "Tell me about your week."

"Joe almost got arrested," Colton announced proudly, like he was reporting breaking news.

Funny, that detail didn't make it into the daily letters.

"Hey!" Joe protested. "Of all the stuff that happened this week, *that's* the first thing you think to tell her?"

"Don't listen to Colton," Royce said. "The police didn't even make Joe get out of the car."

I blinked. I had not mentally prepared for "Joe's brush with the law" to be on today's agenda. But Joe just put his elbow on the table, rested his forehead in his hand, and snort-laughed like this was the funniest thing he'd heard all week.

Should I be concerned? Or assume Colton was exaggerating, as usual?

I asked, "What happened?"

"I want to hear the kids' version first," Joe said.

Simone took that as her cue. "The police lady said he was danger."

Not "a" danger or dangerous. Just danger.

Joe grinned and said with a British accent, "Danger's my middle name, Baby." That was a line from *Austin Powers*. We'd watch the movie together at his house when we were teenagers. I used to giggle when he said the line. Even then, "Caution" would have been a more fitting middle name. I didn't giggle or even smile this time.

"She also said I was little," Royce complained. "So, you can't believe everything she said."

Joe must have seen my concern. He reached across the table and patted my hand that was holding Royce's. "It wasn't as bad as they make it out to be."

"What did you do?" I demanded.

"It's no big deal. I got a ticket for speeding after we left here last week. I can take a defensive driving course online to get it dismissed."

I think he left out some details. "What was that about being dangerous?"

Royce pulled his hand away and put both hands on his hips. "Because I didn't have a booster seat," he said.

Joe groaned and elaborated, "The officer said it was child endangerment."

Okay. That's not so bad. I know Royce is supposed to be in a booster seat, but he's been doing fine without one for months. I blessed Joe with a little smile at his confession.

"And she said I was too little to ride in the front," Royce said in a tone that signaled his irritation. Then he threw in, "I bet she doesn't even have kids."

"Then Joe drove really slow the rest of the way home," Simone tattled.

"Like my grandpa," he said. "One mile under the speed limit."

He squeezed my hand and said, "I wasn't planning on getting another car just yet, but I'm starting to look for one that will fit three booster seats."

I winced at causing one more complexity in his life. "Thank you."

"I'm just trying to stay out of jail," he said with a grin.

Simone blurted out, "We went swimming yesterday," before Joe cut her off.

"Shh. Before we tell your mommy about our playdate, your mommy should tell us something about her week."

I had plenty I could talk about, but it was mostly complaining about things I dared not discuss with so many listeners in the visitation room. Who knows what tidbits might make their way back to inmates or guards who could give me a hard time.

I led with a mild one. "Did y'all go to church this morning?"

Colton answered for the group, "Yeah. My Sunday school teacher prayed for you again."

"Well, I went to church this morning, too," I announced.

"They let you out of jail?" Simone asked.

"No. They have church here."

Simone gave me that look of disbelief. "In jail?"

"Yes. They have a chapel room, and we had singing and preaching."

I leaned toward Joe and lowered my voice to say, "I think half the people go because they're bored."

"Was that the highlight of the week?" he asked.

"Well, that and the naked girl fight."

That caught Royce's interest. "A naked girl was fighting?"

"Two naked girls," I corrected. "Grownup girls, not kids. But I want to hear more of what you did during the week before I tell you about the fight. I heard you drew on the walls."

I glanced at Joe before asking, "Was Joe mad?"

"A little," Royce said.

"I told him to get over it," Colton said.

I chuckled at his comment.

"I don't remember that," Joe said. "But once I found out my mom would paint the place and I didn't have to, I was better."

Simone said, "I painted, too."

"I wish I could've seen your art in person," I told her.

Simone said, "I already covered it up," as if she did all the painting herself.

"Joma did most of it," Royce said. "And me and Colton helped some after school.

I looked at Joe and said, "I bet the white looks nicer than the gray."

Simone said, "It looks happier."

"More pictures are on the way," Joe promised.

"Ethan's mom gave us a picture yesterday," Royce said. "More like a poster."

That seemed odd. "A picture of what?"

"Of you," Colton and Royce said at the same time.

I looked at Joe for further explanation.

"I wanted the kids to have a recent photo of you," Joe said, "so I asked if any of the BIA parents happened to get a picture of you, and Lina was the only one who responded."

Simone said, "We went to their house for swimming."

"Apartment, actually," Joe explained. "She invited us over for a swim."

"All the BIA kids?" I asked.

"No. Just us. I think she was offering us a diversion since she knew you were away."

And she knew Joe merely saw me as a sister. Should I be appreciative?

"Joe thought Hayley was drowning," Simone said. "And he jumped in the water to save her. But she was just showing me how long she could hold her breath."

Joe shrugged his shoulders. "I thought I was properly concerned. Lina thought I was overreacting."

"Aw," I expressed in sympathy. "You got your clothes wet for nothing."

"I was in a swimsuit anyway," he said. "Lina too."

"So, you got to see Lina in a swimsuit," I said. "I bet you were excited about that."

Joe frowned, then quickly changed to a smirk. "How do you know she wasn't excited to see *me* in a swimsuit? Maybe she wanted to see my six-pack abs and impressive biceps." He held up his arms in a bodybuilder pose.

He's cute and generally fit, but I don't think anyone would create an elaborate plan to see him in a swimsuit. I wouldn't look away, though.

I dismissed the image of him in a swimsuit and asked, "Do you think she's hot?"

Before Joe could answer, Royce said, "Alex's dad does. Alex told me."

Why did I ask that? The only satisfying answer would be "no." But I remember how the dads at the campout looked at her in her little denim shorts.

Joe added to Royce's comment. "That's probably why Alex's dad came down to join us. He lives in the complex." Then Joe taunted me with, "He saw the flames from Lina's smoking hot bikini and wanted to see it up close."

I could believe that about Alex's dad, but Joe still didn't give me his opinion. I would have crossed my arms if Colton and Simone weren't on my lap.

I tried to hit the topic from a different angle. "Do you like her?"

"She's just a friend and a good resource for childcare tips," he said with an expression I couldn't read. "Now, your turn," he said. "You owe us the story of the naked girl fight."

"Yeah, Momma," Colton said. "What happened?"

I know what Joe did. He changed the topic to something my kids would rally around. I sighed. "Two women had just gotten out of the shower the other night when they started arguing."

Royce perked up. "What was it about?"

"One woman had something, and the other one wanted it."

"Like… shampoo?" Simone asked.

I ignored her and continued. "They were slapping and scratching and pulling hair. Bouncing off the walls and sinks like pinballs. The guards could barely get them under control because everyone was wet and slippery. It was like watching angry otters fight. They got sent to solitary."

I did *not* mention the knot on my head or the bruise on my back from when they slammed me into the wall. I saw stars and ended up sitting on the disgusting floor until the guards broke it up. No need to traumatize the kids with that part.

"All while naked," Joe added, with way more enthusiasm than necessary.

I leaned toward him, and he leaned in too, like we were about to share state secrets. I whispered, "They weren't as hot as Lina."

As much as I loved having my kids piled on me like emotional support animals, I wished I could talk to Joe alone. With him, I could be a little more graphic – like the part where the infirmary checked me for a concussion, or how I live in constant fear of accidentally offending someone who collects enemies like trading cards.

A guard approached to tell us our time was up. I moved Colton and Simone off my lap and stood to give everyone their final hugs.

"Wait," Royce said. "You didn't tell us what they were fighting over."

"Tampons, honey. One accused the other of stealing her last tampon."

Royce's face went blank, as if I'd just spoken ancient Greek. The guard motioned for me to move.

"What's a tampon?" he asked.

I looked at Joe and grinned. "Ask Joe. I love y'all. Bye."

The door closed behind me, but not before I heard Royce ask, "Joe, what's a tampon?"

And that, honestly, made my whole week.

CHAPTER 39

Joe

I heard Colton cry out from his bedroom in the wee hours of the morning. I ran down the hall to see what the matter was and to keep him from waking up the others.

He lay in bed, eyes closed, and whimpered, "Leave us alone!"

"He's having a bad dream," Royce said. So much for not waking up the others.

I placed my hand on Colton's shoulder and gently shook it, saying, "Colton, Colton. Wake up."

He sat up and grabbed my neck, burying his face in my shirt. Sobbing, he said, "Bad guys were chasing me."

I sounded, "Shh, shh, shh," then assured, "It's not real."

After taking him to the bathroom and checking his closet to prove no bad guys or monsters were hiding in it, I sat on the floor beside his bed, holding him in my lap. I planned to put him back in his bed when he became drowsy again.

At the distant sound of my alarm going off, I woke up on the floor of the boys' bedroom with a crick in my neck and no boys in sight. The light from their bedroom crept its way down the hall and around the corner to provide just enough illumination to the living room for me to see them sleeping on the floor under the poster of Audrey.

I stared at the poster for a few seconds, its features barely visible in the dim pre-dawn light. I carefully stepped between the boys and leaned closer to it as if proximity would allow me to see Audrey. Then for reasons I can't explain, I put both hands on the wall on each side of the poster and kissed Audrey's face, something Simone had been doing nightly.

"I miss you, too," I told poster Audrey.

* * *

The trip to the BIA campout was the inaugural run for our newly acquired, ten-year-old, very damaged van. That's not counting the drive home from the repair shop where Audrey's mother worked. Two weeks ago, I came across an auto accident on the way home. A pickup truck had collided with a Mount Ebenezer Baptist Church van, and had traffic backed up for blocks as three lanes had to squeeze into one to get past.

No one was seriously injured, as far as I could tell, but the van didn't look drivable. The next morning, I called Audrey's mother to ask whether she got an employee discount on auto repairs. I described the damage, and she checked with mechanics at the shop on the possibility of making it roadworthy again. We struck a deal: I would buy the crippled van, she would cover the repairs, and Audrey would take title. If Audrey ever sold it, she and I would split the money.

I bought the junker from the church's insurance company for cheap. They wrote up the vehicle as totaled. The insurance representative explained that the truck drove through a red light and plowed into the passenger side of the van. They confirmed no serious injuries, but the van was a mess. Both vehicles tried to swerve to avoid a direct T-bone collision, which would have caused damage beyond repair. As it was, the passenger sliding door, front door, and front fender were badly smashed, and the front right wheel was turned at an impossible angle. With the vehicle's age and mileage, the cost of repair exceeded the value. I applied for a salvage title.

When Beverly called to tell me the work was done, I drove to her shop straight from the office. Masterson Automotive was a local chain whose employees prided themselves on the immaculate cleanliness of their repair shops, a big contrast to her husband's shop, which I recall had grease smears on the floors, doors, and the front desk countertop. She met me at the shop with the kids.

Colton looked at me with disappointment. "I thought you were smart," he said, in front of his grandmother and the mechanics.

"You don't think so?" I asked.

"Nana said you bought a van. And when we got here, that's what it is," he said, pointing to the white van sitting in the parking lot. It was taller and longer than the vehicles on either side, a mid-roof 15-passenger Ford Transit 350.

Someone had peeled off the labels from the sides and back that had the church name, leaving long rectangles of a brighter white than the rest of the van. No one bothered to remove the labels with the church's motto.

Colton pointed to the label and asked, "What does that say?"

"God answers prayer," Royce said.

"Who prayed for a crashed van?" Colton asked. "It's a piece of crap."

Beverly said, "Colton, watch your mouth."

I inwardly smiled at his statement because I agreed with it, but with his grandmother's admonition, I felt compelled to count it as misbehavior. "That's one," I said.

He curled up his lip and crossed his little six-year-old arms.

Simone looked directly at me and said, "It's ugly."

Then I looked at Royce. "Are you gonna weigh in?"

He shrugged his shoulders. "It means we're poor. We've always been poor."

"You kids need to be nice," Beverly told them. "It still works, and it will hold all of you with proper booster seats and even has room for friends."

The shop made it drivable, not pretty. They replaced the damaged fender with a gray one but didn't do anything about the doors with their massive dents. The mechanic handed me the key and gave me the rundown, which I'd already heard before the repairs.

"We replaced the wheel assembly and an engine mount, gave it an alignment, and changed the oil," he said. He ran his hand across damaged doors. "Beverly's son found the fender at a salvage yard. Don't try to open the doors on this side. The center column is bent, and if you manage to get 'em open, you probably won't be able to close 'em. I also disconnected the wires to the power window. It would go down about an inch but wouldn't go back up."

"How much did the repairs cost?" I asked.

Beverly held up a hand. "That's not your business. I've got a sale pending on the house, so I'll have plenty to cover it."

"If the doors don't work, how do we get in?" Royce asked.

The mechanic motioned us to follow him to the back of the vehicle.

"From here," he said, opening a back door. "We took out the back row of seats to give you access to the aisle. It also gives you some cargo space."

"Room for camping gear," I said, looking at the boys.

"Those side doors don't seal very well," the mechanic pointed out. "I recommend you spray some foam sealant in the cracks to keep out the noise and rain."

I nodded my acknowledgment. "I appreciate your effort."

Simone reiterated, "It's ugly."

"It's just what we need," I told her.

* * *

Friday evening, I got home early to go to the BIA campout, the Halloween Campout, as the Chapter called it. I found the van covered with large stickers of jack-o'-lanterns, scarecrows, and cartoonish ghosts, courtesy of Beverly.

We loaded our camping gear in the back and drove to Huntsville State Park. Simone and Colton sat in the row directly behind me; Royce sat three rows back. At least he started there. After trying to hold a conversation from such a distance over the sound of the road noise coming in through the ill-fitting doors, he unbuckled himself and moved with his new booster seat to the single chair opposite the aisle from his siblings and one row behind them.

"You're not supposed to be changing seats while we're driving," I scolded. Both boys wore their uniforms, making this an official BIA trip. "Remember, we're on a mission. That means you have to obey the safety rules."

"It's okay, Joe," he said, as if that really made it okay. "Nothing happened."

* * *

As last time, several families had arrived early at the campsite and set up their tents. Some had glowing plastic jack-o'-lanterns set outside their tents in the spirit of the season.

The boys and I set up our tent while Simone shadowed Lina's daughter, Hayley, at their tent. After the tent was up and our gear stowed inside, I released the boys to mingle with their crews while I set up the kids' cots and inflated my air mattress with a pump plugged into a portable power station I'd borrowed from Dad. Simone ran up excitedly with Hayley right behind.

"Joe! Hayley said I can have a sleepover in their tent tonight. Miss Lina said I had to ask you."

Lina arrived a few seconds later.

"Are you sure about this?" I asked.

"We can swap kids," she said. "I'll take Simone, and you take Ethan. He'd rather be with you guys than with us girls, anyway."

Her reasoning made sense. "Okay, I'm fine with that."

Simone and Hayley cheered and ran off to tell the boys. Two minutes later, Mark, Royce's crew chief, came over.

"I heard the boys say Ethan was staying with Royce this weekend."

"Yeah. I'm taking Ethan and…," I said, then nodded toward Lina, "she's taking Simone."

"We'll have a girls' tent and a boys' tent," Lina explained.

"I'm not opposed to the idea," Mark said, "but it's against BIA rules. The boys can only stay with their own parent, or in your case, Joe, guardian."

Lina and I exchanged looks of disappointment mixed with irritation.

"It's a legal issue," Mark explained. "Aunts, uncles, and grandparents are okay, but not another boy's parent." He looked at Lina and said, "I can't stop Royce's sister from staying with you, since she's not an official member of the BIA. But…." He looked back at me and let his voice trail off. He finished with a shrug.

Lina restated Mark's position. "So, Ethan has to stay in a tent with me, and Royce has to stay in a tent with Joe."

"That's right," Mark confirmed.

Lina poked her head in one side of my two-room tent, then in the other. The divider wall was translucent enough that my electric lantern illuminated both rooms, albeit the lantern side brighter than the other.

"And if both families are in the same tent?" Lina asked.

Mark opened his mouth, but the only sound that came out was, "Um." It took a moment for the words to follow. "I, uh, … I'll have to check."

Lina looked at me with a smile, "I've heard you're generous with your spare bedrooms."

"I do have that reputation," I admitted.

Her plan surprised me, but I admired her ability to find a loophole. It must be her legal background.

Mark looked as if he had more to say but again had trouble finding the words. Finally, he said, "You know this chapter is sponsored by a church. Don't embarrass us."

Lina gasped and said, "Mark, do you think Joe and I will be hooking up in the middle of a campout full of kids? Especially our own kids? We'll be sleeping on separate sides of the divider!"

After Mark walked away, she covered her mouth and tried to stifle her laugh. She failed.

"I think we're going to be the subject of rumors," she said with a giggle.

"Definitely," I noted. "I'm sure Alex's dad will be disappointed."

"Are you implying something between Grant and me?"

"Oh, like you and him don't have something going on?"

"We live in the same complex. Sometimes our kids play together. That's it."

My response was a shrug. I heard what she said, but I'm not sure I believed it. If I remember correctly from the pool day, Grant knew which cabinet in her kitchen held the cups and which drawer had the forks.

"Need help bringing your stuff over?" I asked.

Mark didn't talk to us again that night, so he must not have found a BIA rule against two families sharing a tent. Alex's dad issued a heavy sigh when I saw him later that evening.

CHAPTER 40

Audrey

The boys looked so adorable in their BIA uniforms, but I kept that opinion to myself. Royce would have died on the spot, and Colton would've given me about eighteen seconds of tolerance before deciding affection was "embarrassing." I might have one more year with him before he joins the Brotherhood of Too-Cool Sons.

We did our usual round of hugs after settling at the visitation table, but I froze when it was Simone's turn.

"What's that dark stuff smeared on your face?" I asked, already bracing for the worst.

"Chocolate," Joe said, pulling a napkin from his pocket like a magician revealing his next trick. He started scrubbing her cheeks with the weary precision of a man who has cleaned this exact child's face approximately nine thousand times.

"We did trickle treat at the campout," Simone announced proudly.

She still says *trickle treat*, and I refuse to correct her. It's adorable, and I'm hoarding every scrap of adorable I can get right now. I wish I could've been there. I miss them so much it aches.

Once the chocolate threat to my white prison shirt had been neutralized, I kissed her cheek and squeezed her tight. Not a Joe squeeze. Just a regular mom hug.

"We got to wear our Halloween costumes," Colton said.

Royce muttered, "But not the cool ones."

Joe chuckled. "He means, they couldn't wear scary costumes. Some of the older boys complained that they couldn't dress as zombies or victims of a serial killer. They'll have to save those for actual Halloween. For the campout, they had to settle for superheroes, historical figures, or princesses."

He paused before adding, "Uh, that last one was for the sisters, not the boys."

"Yeah, I figured out that part," I said.

Royce rolled his eyes. Seeing an eight-year-old do that when it wasn't directed at me looked almost as cute as Simone's trickle treat.

"Remind me what your costumes were," I said. We'd discussed Halloween costumes last week, but I wanted to hear it again.

"I went as Spiderman," Colton stated proudly. "Joe didn't let me wear it today."

"You had to wear your BIA shirt on the drive," Joe said, matter-of-factly.

I remember that rule from the last campout. Wear the button-up uniform shirt for the drive. And when they got to the campground, they could change into their green BIA T-shirt for activities that might involve sweat and dirt.

"I wanted to go as a skeleton with light-up bones, but…." Royce looked at Joe as he continued, "I went as an astronaut."

"I thought skeletons might fall into the scary category," Joe said.

"Not if they light up," Royce complained.

"I hope you took pictures," I told them. Well, that was mainly for Joe.

"I did," he confirmed. "I'll print them as soon as we get home and have them in the mail tomorrow," he promised.

I turned to Simone. "Did you stick with the mermaid costume?"

"No. I dressed like a cat, like Hayley."

"Well, a mercat," Joe said.

It sounded like he said muhr-cat, not meercat. That wasn't a term I was familiar with. "Mercat?"

"Like a mermaid, but for a cat," Joe explained. "Mercat. Lina brought extra cat ears and painted cat makeup on the girls. You know, black nose, whiskers, and that little line under the nose. Simone still wore the mermaid dress, though. But she liked what Lina and Hayley were doing."

"Lina, huh?" I said. "Sounds like you're spending a lot of time with Lina lately."

"She's just being nice," Joe defended.

"They stayed with us," Simone announced, blowing his defense to pieces like a tiny, cheerful whistleblower.

I blinked. "What do you mean?"

Royce, bless his honest little soul, confessed. "Ethan and Hayley and Miss Lina stayed in our tent."

It felt like someone had just informed me my jail sentence got extended for bad attitude. I pressed my lips together and gave Joe the kind of glare that could peel paint.

He started talking faster, which is Joe-speak for *Let me finish before you explode.* "Simone wanted a sleepover with Hayley, and Ethan wanted to stay with Royce, and the only way to do that within BIA rules is if both families stay in the same tent."

I kept glaring. "There's actually a rule for that?"

"It's more like the absence of a rule," he said. "A gap between other rules against kids staying with adults from another family."

Sure. I think he was inventing legislation on the spot.

Royce asked, "Momma, are you okay?"

"Yeah, Honey. My stomach just feels a little funny today, but I'm fine." Funny as in *I might throw up on your father figure.*

Simone jumped in. "Nana let me put Halloween stickers on the van."

Joe hissed a "shh" at her, which was adorable because Simone has never once in her life been shushable.

"Nana got a van?" I asked.

"No. *We* did," Simone said. "A big one."

Joe sighed the sigh of a man who has accepted defeat. "Simone, you can't keep anything secret, can you?"

"No, she can't," Royce confirmed. "She tells Momma everything."

Sometimes that's a blessing. Sometimes it's a grenade.

"So," I said sweetly, "are we talking about the secret of getting a van or the secret of spending the night with Lina?"

Joe groaned. "Stop obsessing over Lina. It's not a big deal. She and the girls stayed on one side of the wall, and the boys and I stayed on the other. Same as with you and me last time. She's just a BIA mom whose kids like to play with our kids – your kids."

I caught the slip. *Our* kids. Normally that would've made my heart do a little cartwheel, but the whole Lina situation had my heart sitting in the corner with its arms crossed.

"You should consider her your friend, too," Joe said. "Two single moms trying to raise their kids alone."

It hadn't felt so alone those last few months. But it feels pretty alone now.

* * *

I dreamed again that I was back on the lake in my father's ski boat with Dad, Liam, and Joe. As in the last dream, Dad drove the boat the way a toddler draws with crayons—wild, chaotic, and with no regard for the people involved. One sharp swerve and Joe went flying into the water. Another swerve and I followed.

Once more, we bobbed in the lake, yards apart, when the sleek speedboat zoomed up beside Joe. And who leaned over to rescue him? Lina, of course. She reached out, all slow-motion and heroic, and pulled him aboard like she was starring in *Baywatch: BIA Mom Edition*.

"Joe! Joe!" I yelled, splashing like a drowning duck.

Lina gave me a cheerful little wave as they sped off toward the distant shore, leaving me behind to be swept dramatically toward the giant waterfall over the dam.

Even my subconscious thinks I'm the understudy in my own love story.

CHAPTER 41

Joe

The kids had some rough spots with behavior in the first week or two of Audrey's incarceration. More tantrums and fights than they had in the weeks before. And I admit I had my meltdowns, too, mostly about their meltdowns. Then we all had a timeout, even me, and it got better.

One of the worst was the fight over Nana's popsicles. She'd brought a box of them over. They'd eaten three – one for each kid – the afternoon she brought them. The next night, they hounded me to let them each have another. It had been a long day for me, and I was weak-willed. I checked the box in the freezer. There should have been three remaining in the 6-count box. But I found only two. Simone grabbed a red one and ran to the far end of the kitchen to quickly unwrap it and plunge it into her mouth. That left me holding the one remaining popsicle.

"Why is there only one left!?" Royce demanded.

"It's mine!" Colton yelled, reaching for it.

I held it out of his reach until I could sort out the mystery of the missing popsicle or determine if one of the boys would be willing to go without.

Royce looked at me and said through clenched teeth, "Did you eat the other one?"

"Absolutely not," I said, although I'm not sure he believed me.

Colton went to the kitchen trash can and began pulling out trash. Dirty paper towels, an empty box of macaroni and cheese, and the empty carton from our heat-and-serve dinner lasagna.

"Colton! What are you doing?" I asked.

He held up the clear plastic wrapper with the logo of the popsicle brand. "Finding this."

He stared at me defiantly for a moment, then looked at his siblings. "Who ate it!?" he demanded.

Then both boys looked at Simone.

"You ate Royce's popsicle!" Colton shouted.

I'm not sure Royce agreed with Colton about the ownership of the treat, but they both rushed Simone, who plucked the treat out of her mouth as she ran into the living room.

Through screaming, chasing, and hair-pulling, the slimy red popsicle flew through the air, hit the newly painted white wall, and broke in two as it slid to the floor, leaving a streak of red.

I yelled, "Go to your rooms! Now!"

So much for enacting discipline without emotions. After I put the remaining popsicle back in the freezer and cleaned up the mess in the living room, I sent myself to time out.

That was days ago, and everyone's been better since then. A few shouting matches, but overall better. Until an altercation with some kids from another street that occurred before I got home. Royce had a bruise on his cheek, and Colton had a scrape on his arm, which sported two adhesive bandages adorned in a green, brown, and beige camouflage pattern. They did a poor job of camouflaging anything. Beverly said the boys got into a fight with some other kids.

"They were from another street," Colton elaborated. "They're always rude."

Neither of us adults knew enough about the circumstances to enact discipline.

That night, when the doorbell rang, I opened the door to find a mother I didn't recognize standing with a girl of about six or seven whom I also didn't recognize. The woman's expression indicated she'd come on business. Serious business.

"I'm Taylor Westfield from around the corner," she said.

The girl, who had been somewhat hiding behind her mother, pointed beyond me and said, "That's him."

I turned to see all three kids standing behind me. Royce gave a little wave and said, "Hey, Livvy."

When she moved out from behind her mother to point, I couldn't help but notice the bandage on her chin. A strip of medical tape holding a gauze pad. I took a deep breath and asked Ms. Westfield, "What did he do?"

"What's your name?" she asked, making me wonder if she needed it for the lawsuit.

"Uh, sorry. I'm Joe. Joe Sanders."

Then she looked at Royce and repeated her question. "And what's your name?"

"Royce."

"I'm Colton," Colton volunteered.

Not to be left out, Simone added, "I'm Simone."

"Royce," she said, pausing long enough for me to wonder what crime she was about to accuse him of. "Thank you."

That was unexpected.

"I'm impressed with your son," she said. "You should be proud." Her facial expressions didn't seem to go with her words, making me wonder if she was being sarcastic.

I looked at Royce and then back at Ms. Westfield. Perhaps she sensed my confusion.

"Didn't they tell you what happened?"

"No. I only understand there was a fight," I told her.

"Those other boys made her fall off her bike," Colton said. "We saw it."

"Yeah," Royce agreed. "They ride our bus, and they're always messing with the little kids."

"They're in fourth grade," Ms. Westfield explained. "And Livvy's had run-ins with them before."

"We chased them away," Royce said. "One of them shoved Colton, and he fell on the sidewalk, and then I hit that boy, and he hit me back. But then they ran away."

I may not be his father, as Livvy's mother assumed, but at that moment, I truly was proud of the boys for standing up for themselves and someone else.

Ms. Westfield finally smiled as she looked directly at Royce. "You left out the most important part."

"What?" he asked.

She looked at me to explain, "When Livvy fell off her bike, she hit her chin on the curb. Royce wiped the blood away with his shirt and bandaged up her chin. He's our little hero."

To emphasize the point, Royce pulled another adhesive bandage from a pocket of his cargo shorts. "Mr. Mark said we should always be prepared."

"Well, the urgent care doctor said you did the right thing," Ms. Westfield said.

I didn't know he carried first aid supplies with him. How long has he been doing that?

"We're in Boys in Action," he said. "We help people."

"Me, too," Colton added as if the 'we' didn't convey that point.

Simone said, "I'm gonna be in Boys in Action someday."

That was not the time to correct her understanding of the boys-only group.

"Did she get stitches?" Royce asked.

"No, they glued it shut," Ms. Westfield said.

"Glue?" he asked in amazement.

I stared at Royce, trying to process the events they just described. Fending off bullies. Rendering first aid.

Ms. Westfield broke me out of my frozen state when she said, "Royce, we are very grateful. Livvy has a present for you."

The girl held out a paper bag to Royce and said, "We made cookies for you." When Royce took the bag, Livvy stepped forward and hugged him.

Later that evening, I found Royce's dark blue T-shirt on the floor of his closet, its dark color masking the blood stains, likely why his grandmother didn't mention the fight resulted in spilled blood.

Yes, I was proud of Royce. Colton, too.

* * *

On our final visit to Audrey in jail, the boys excitedly talked over each other, describing their battle to save the damsel on our street from evil forces and then treating her wounds. Simone described the cookies. Chocolate chip.

Audrey seemed more distant with me. Did she blame me for the boys getting into a fight? I told her I was proud of them and left it at that. At least she didn't take it out on them. I didn't want to distract from the kids' visit with her to argue. I'd be picking her up in a few days anyway, and if it still bothered her, we could discuss it then.

Her last words to me before leaving were, "Say hello to Lina for me."

CHAPTER 42

Audrey

I don't know why they had to schedule my release for the afternoon. Why not do all releases in the morning so we could skip one last prison lunch? But no – 2:30 p.m. was my official "you may now leave the premises" time. Bureaucracy loves suffering.

During discharge, they offered me elastic-waist blue jeans, a gray polo, and black canvas slip-ons. Basically the "Congratulations, You're Free" starter pack. I took the shoes and declined the rest, choosing to wear the same clothes I'd worn to court a month ago. Nothing says "fresh start" like stale laundry.

I walked out carrying a cheap tote bag stuffed with letters, photos, and the dress shoes and underwear I'd worn to court. Very glamorous.

I half-hoped my mom would be waiting, with or without Joe. I fully expected to see Joe tapping his foot like a man who'd been forced to listen to hold music for twenty minutes. As I approached the door, I peeked through the window.

No Mom. Just Joe.

He was talking to an elderly woman, his back turned, but I recognized the box-print dress shirt I'd ironed a thousand times. After all the Lina talk, I braced myself for a lukewarm, "Hey, glad you're not incarcerated anymore." He turned when I opened the door.

And he had flowers.

"You look good," he said, stepping forward.

I froze, unsure how to greet him. A few weeks ago, I'd imagined bursting into the arms of loved ones like a Hallmark movie. But it was a school day, so Mom was probably at the bus stop. And Joe and I weren't lovers. While I was rotting in jail, he'd apparently been bonding with Lina, proving he wasn't allergic to single moms – just to me.

He held out the bouquet, but as I reached for it, he switched gears and leaned in for a hug. Naturally, that was the exact moment another inmate was discharged behind me, and a woman in the waiting area yelled, "Y'all move out of the way!"

Joe gave a sheepish smile and aborted the hug, stepping aside like a gentleman who'd been scolded by a stranger. Once the path was clear, he handed me the flowers and took my tote. At his Camry, he opened the door for me. He hadn't done that since high school, back when chivalry was still alive and not on life support.

He started the engine. "How do you feel?"

"Relieved," I said. Then added, "I'll feel even better once we get out of the parking lot." As if the guards might sprint out, shout "Oops, wrong inmate!" and drag me back inside.

The flowers smelled... well, flowery. Peach roses, pink carnations, blue asters, lavender chrysanthemums, pink alstroemeria. No red roses, the universal symbol of romance. Message received.

"Oh, I almost forgot," he said as we waited for an eighteen-wheeler to lumber past. He reached into the backseat and pulled out a Burger King paper crown. He placed it on my head. "I declare today, Audrey Freedom Day!"

I flipped down the visor mirror and adjusted my royal headwear. I laughed. "You didn't have to do that. And you didn't have to get me flowers."

"I didn't have to. I wanted to. It's nice to hear you laugh. Oh – and one more thing..."

He opened the center console, pulled out a Ziploc bag, and handed it to me. Inside were all my piercings and rings – ear, nose, dimple, finger rings. My entire former personality in a sandwich bag.

"I thought you didn't like my piercings," I said.

"When did I ever say that?"

"You thought it real loud."

"Today's not about me. It's about you. If you're into face piercings, I'm fine with it."

The first few days in jail, I kept touching my face like something was missing – because something *was* missing. But after a few weeks, I stopped thinking about them. The holes had started to close, the dimple dents filling in. They used to be part of who I was. Now... I wasn't sure.

I dropped the bag into my tote. "And what if I don't want them anymore?"

Did he just... smile?

"Totally up to you."

"I knew you didn't like them!"

"How did you get that conclusion?"

"You smiled. It was quick, but I saw it."

"I don't know what you're talking about."

Fifteen minutes later, Joe's phone rang through the speakers. "Beverly Harris," the screen flashed.

Mom.

Joe answered, and I said, "Hi, Mom."

Instead of Mom's voice, all three kids erupted like a pack of caffeinated squirrels: "Mommy!" "Are you out?" "When are you coming home?"

Mom laughed in the background. "We all missed you."

And for the first time in a month, I felt I could breathe again.

CHAPTER 43

Joe

I expected Audrey to show more excitement when I picked her up. Maybe she would come bounding out with a huge smile; bounce a little like another newly released inmate did a few minutes before Audrey came out. Maybe, just maybe, fling herself into my arms.

I didn't realize how much I would miss her until she was gone. Not because of the chores that fell back onto my shoulders, or the extra duties I took on for her kids. Those were big issues. Huge, even. But I mostly missed her presence. I missed our dinner conversations, as trivial as they often were. I missed her humor. I missed her hugs before bed.

My initial disappointment in Audrey's muted reaction dissipated on the ride home. She still didn't seem fully relaxed, and I wondered if this was how a caged animal felt upon release into the wild, assessing the environment to confirm if it was safe and the release was real. At least she kept the crown on.

I passed the driveway and pulled up to the curb in front of the house, behind our mothers' cars. This occasion called for entering through the front door like a VIP. Audrey reached for the door handle, and I stopped her.

"Wait. I'll come around."

The door of the house opened, and the kids came bounding out with our moms following behind. I barely made it to Audrey's side of the car before the kids did.

"Stand back," I told them as I opened the car door.

The kids latched onto her and wouldn't let go. I pried Royce away and got him to carry the tote and flowers. Then I straightened the paper crown on Audrey's head and pushed the small crowd toward the house, the younger kids holding their mom's hands as they moved.

* * *

Mom searched for a vase for the flowers as Audrey looked around the living room. The flowers found their way into a water pitcher in the center of the breakfast table.

"It looks different," Audrey said of the living room.

"Brighter?" my mother asked, fishing for validation of her redecorating efforts.

"Yeah, brighter, cleaner," Audrey said. "It's the new paint! The white looks cleaner than that old gray."

"We painted all the rooms," Royce said. "We all helped. Well, everyone except Joe."

"Hey!" I objected. "I had to work every day. Someone's got to make money to pay for all this. Besides, I painted the fireplace."

"Y'all did a good job," Audrey said, hugging Simone and Colton tighter. They hadn't left her side since she got home.

She looked more closely at the fireplace, perhaps due to my last statement, then walked over and picked up the prom photo. She looked at me and said, "Where did you find this?"

I nodded to her mother and said, "She found it."

"When I was packing up to move," Beverly explained. "It was in one of the boxes in your old closet."

"Mommy, look at the other picture," Simone said, pointing behind Audrey.

CHAPTER 44

Audrey

I turned and found myself face-to-face with… myself. Well, almost. Poster-me wasn't looking at *me* so much as staring suspiciously down the hallway, like she'd heard a noise and was about to call 911. I gasped out a little laugh and covered my mouth. Joe's smirk said he'd been waiting for that reaction.

"Is that from the campout?" I asked.

"Yep," he said. "Lina's gift to the kids. When I came home from work that Monday, it was already hanging there. Mom bought a frame and everything."

Lina really was everywhere these days. Was this her strategy? Seduce Joe by giving him a life-size poster of *me*? That's… creative. And deeply unsettling.

Colton walked up to the poster and pressed his face against poster-me's stomach, arms stretched wide like he was hugging a refrigerator. "This is how we say good night to you."

"Sometimes Joe holds me up so I can kiss your face," Simone added.

And right on cue, Joe scooped her up and held her next to my *actual* face. Simone kissed my cheek like she was demonstrating proper technique for a class.

Joe set her down. "Dad's coming over between five-thirty and six, and then I thought we could all go to Frida's Fajitas to celebrate."

I must not have looked thrilled. Probably because I was still processing the fact that my children had been kissing a poster of me like I was a celebrity cardboard cutout at a movie theater.

Mom swooped in. "Oh, Honey, you're overwhelmed, aren't you? We can pick up something and eat here. We're just so happy you're out."

"No, it's not that," I said. "I just really want a shower. A long one."

I leaned toward Mom and whispered, "I haven't shaved my legs or armpits in a while. I want to go out, but not like this."

She did *not* whisper back. "Honey, no one can see your hairy armpits and legs."

Ms. Joanna smiled politely. Joe raised his eyebrows like he'd just learned something he wished he hadn't.

"Maybe so," I said, "but *I* know. I need to do it."

"We have plenty of time," Joe said. "All your stuff is still in the bathroom where you left it." Then he turned to the group. "Y'all wait here. Give her some space."

Naturally, he did not give me space. He followed me to my bedroom.

He went to the closet and came out holding a fluffy white bathrobe and matching slippers like he was presenting offerings to a queen. "I got these for you. The good kind like at fancy hotels. And bubble bath. And scented candles. I thought you might want to relax in the tub after you got home. But maybe now's not a good time."

I leaned in close, checking his face for a zipper or silicone seam. "Who are you, and what did you do with the real Joe?"

* * *

After the shower, instead of going to my vanity area as I would have done at bedtime to brush my teeth, I took a shortcut through Joe's vanity area. His mirror had a little yellow square stuck to the glass near the left side frame. It was a sticky note that had one word scrawled in the middle in blue ink, "Audrey." *Remember to ask Joe about that*, I reminded myself.

I walked to the living room in my new bathrobe to peek at everyone waiting patiently for me.

"I was about to check on you," Mom said. "You were in the shower a long time."

"It was nice not to feel rushed," I said.

"Dad called while you were shaving your armpits," Joe said with a smirk. He glanced at his watch. "He'll be here in about ten minutes."

I looked around at the small group in our living room. He would be the eighth person. "He could just meet us at Frida's," I suggested. "We'll need multiple cars anyway."

Mom chuckled. "She hasn't seen the van yet, has she?"

Joe grinned. "I don't think she was paying attention when we drove up."

"Mom! Mom!" Royce shouted excitedly. "Come see it!"

"Let her get dressed first," Joe told him.

CHAPTER 45

Joe

Dinner at Frida's was supposed to be a fun celebration of Audrey's release, and it started that way. Audrey wore a dress that was more suitable for warmer weather, one that showed her smooth legs. She even submitted to wearing the Burger King crown at Simone's insistence. The interaction between Simone and the waitress only set her back temporarily.

"I like your crown," the waitress told Audrey. "Are we celebrating something? A birthday, maybe?"

Simone cleared that idea right up. She cheerily said, "Mommy got out of jail today."

The poor waitress didn't know how to react to that one. She froze for a second, then stammered, "Oh. Um. Okay."

Audrey looked at Simone, then at me with wide eyes and a fake smile, like she blamed me for Simone's announcement.

Dad broke the tension with his request to the waitress, "Let's celebrate with some sopapillas before the meal."

After the sweet appetizer and piles of beef and chicken fajitas, Audrey perked up again. That is, until she caught me texting near the end of our meal.

"Who's that?" she asked.

"Lina," I said. "She's asking if we'll still be here when the BIA meeting is over."

"Why?"

"She wants to stop by and welcome you back," I explained. "It's on her way home."

We didn't see Lina that night, but Audrey seemed moody the rest of the evening.

CHAPTER 46

Audrey

Back at the house, our parents left, and everything *should* have snapped back to normal. But nothing felt normal. It was like someone had taken my life, shaken it like a snow globe, and then put everything back *almost* where it belonged – but slightly off, just enough to make me question my sanity.

Same house. Same people. But the walls were white instead of gray, there was a new picture on the mantle, another on the wall, a fall centerpiece of gourds in the dining room, courtesy of Joe's mother, who apparently moonlights as a seasonal décor fairy, and fresh kid artwork on the fridge. None of it was bad. It just wasn't... mine.

And the kids' routines? Completely rearranged.

"I'm sure we'd all love to continue celebrating Mommy being home," Joe said, "but it's a school night, and you kids haven't had baths yet."

Bath reminders were supposed to be *my* job. I'd been replaced by a man who once thought "rinse and repeat" was optional.

"I'm going last," Royce declared. Some things never change.

I nodded and looked at Simone. "That means you're up."

"No," Colton said. "I go first."

I shot Joe a raised eyebrow that translated to: *Excuse me, sir, who authorized this schedule change?* He just smiled and shrugged like a man who had no idea he was playing with fire.

"Alright, buddy," I told Colton. "Let's go."

I followed him to his room to grab pajamas, then turned toward the bathroom. He snatched the pajamas from me like a tiny, polite thief.

"No. I do it myself."

I stood in the hallway, listening to the faucet run. I should've been in there checking the water temperature, making sure he didn't boil himself alive. After a minute, I cracked the door open.

"No, Mommy! Go out! I do it myself now."

I retreated like I'd been caught sneaking into a top-secret meeting.

Joe appeared behind me, making me jump. "He can handle it. Go visit with Royce and Simone."

Then I heard wet feet slap across the tile and the bathroom door shut completely. I pouted. Joe chuckled. At least Simone still needed me. Probably.

While Royce took his bath, I tucked Simone into bed. I started our usual prayer, but she stopped me.

"Where's Joe? He's 'posed to be here."

Joe? *Joe?* Since when was Joe part of bedtime? Pre-jail Joe barely knew where the kids' bedrooms were.

I looked toward the door and saw him standing in the hallway like a stagehand waiting for his cue. He turned off the overhead light and stepped in.

A lump formed in my throat. "You don't want me to tuck you in anymore?"

"You *and* Joe," Simone clarified, with the tone of someone who would absolutely say "Duh" if she were thirteen.

With both of us in position beside her bed – *our* bed – she finally let me start the prayer. She added her own line thanking God that I came home and didn't have to stay with "the bad people in jail anymore." Sweet. Disturbing. Accurate.

I pulled the covers to her chin, kissed her, and whispered, "I love you." Then I stepped back, hoping she'd be asleep by the time I crawled in beside her.

She closed her eyes and murmured, "Joe."

I watched as he leaned in, kissed her forehead, and whispered, "I love you, Sweetie. Good night."

Did Joe hijack my kids while I was gone?

Because it sure felt like he'd staged a very gentle, very wholesome coup.

* * *

Back in the living room, Joe motioned for me to join him on the sofa. The coffee table held two cups of tea, steaming like we were suddenly the kind of people who "unwind" instead of "collapse."

"What's that look?" he asked.

"What look?"

"Like you've never had chamomile tea before."

My look wasn't about the tea. It was about the fact that we were drinking *tea*, period. Hot tea. At night. Like civilized adults. This had literally never happened in the history of us. But instead of pointing that out, I asked, "Is that what this is?"

"Lina suggested it," he said. "It helps you relax and sleep."

"Lina, huh?"

"Yeah. The bubble bath, candle, and lotion were her idea, too."

For him or for me? Hard to tell. I took a polite sip, the kind you take when you're not sure if something is poisoned.

"But the robe and slippers were totally my idea," he added quickly. Then he echoed Simone's earlier line, "I'm glad you're back and don't have to stay with all those bad people in jail."

"I bet you're ready for me to be back."

He took a sip of his tea. "It was weird not having you around."

"No one to do the cooking and cleaning, right? Oh, and the kids. Thanks for taking care of them. They're a handful. Especially when you're on your own."

"It was rough at first," he admitted. "But our mothers helped."

We finished our tea in awkward silence, both of us staring into our cups like the answers to life might be floating in the chamomile. I had a whole month-long saga I didn't know how to explain, and he had… well, Lina's wellness starter kit. How do we even begin that conversation?

* * *

That night, after brushing my teeth in the master bathroom, I told Joe goodnight and went to my room. A few seconds later, I heard a light tapping on the doorframe and turned to see Joe standing in the doorway.

"Hey," he whispered, then walked in like he owned the place.

I met him halfway and whispered back, "What?"

I froze when he slipped his hands around my waist and pulled me close.

"You forgot the hug," he said.

It wasn't that I forgot. I just assumed the nightly hug had expired like a coupon he wasn't interested in redeeming anymore. But after the initial shock, I relaxed and slid my hands up his arms to his shoulders.

Then I remembered the sticky note on his mirror. "You have my name on your bathroom mirror," I said.

I couldn't see his expression in the shadows, but he let out a soft exhale, the kind that sounds suspiciously like a smile trying to escape.

"It was a reminder to pray for you," he said.

He gave me a gentle squeeze, then let go. "Welcome home," he murmured before slipping back to his room.

And I just stood there, wondering why my heart felt like it had been tossed into a blender set to "confuse."

CHAPTER 47

Joe

We spent the next few days trying to return to our old routine. Well, not quite. Audrey had her own set of wheels now, so she could go grocery shopping without me. I gave her a debit card on a bank account I set up for gas, groceries, and other household expenses.

Sunday morning, our Bible class welcomed her back. They all knew where she'd been, but no one asked about it. The closest acknowledgement was from a woman who told her they'd been praying for her safety.

As we came out of church, I heard a familiar voice call out, "Joseph!"

I turned toward the caller to find a balding fifty-something-year-old man in khakis and a dark blue zipper-neck sweater walking with a forty-something woman with dark hair, whom I presumed was his wife. She wore flowing brown pants that I initially mistook for a skirt and a blue denim jacket over a white blouse.

"George?" I said with surprise. "I didn't know you went to church here!" It was a big church.

He grinned at my revelation. "Fifteen years."

I released Simone's hand to shake his. Then I turned to Audrey, "This is George Gillman, my favorite client."

"I'm sure he says that about all his clients," George said.

Before I had a chance to respond, he stuck his hand out to Audrey and said, "You must be the infamous Audrey."

"Yes, I am," she replied, shaking his hand, while giving me the side eye.

George turned to the woman at his side and said, "This is my wife, Trish."

Then he said, "Hon, this is the Joe I used to golf with. Until he got distracted…," he paused and looked at Audrey, "… with other things."

Trish smiled and said, "Nice to meet you both. And who are these with you?"

I pointed to each child as I introduced them, "Royce, Colton, and Simone."

Simone took that as her cue to grab my hand again

"Eight, five, and four," Audrey added.

George asked, "What are y'all doing for lunch?"

I shrugged and looked at Audrey. "Cici's Pizza," I said. We hadn't discussed it, but that had become our go-to lunch place since we started going to church.

"Pizza buffet? I think you can do better than that," George said. "Today you're coming with us to Carousel Cafe." He looked at the kids and said, "They cover the tables with butcher paper and give you crayons to draw on them."

His choice of restaurants was odd. "Aren't your kids grown?" I asked.

"She's a kid at heart," George said, putting his arm around his wife. "Besides, they make the best peppercorn burgers."

"And I get to doodle while we wait for our food," she said.

Then George appealed to my sense of duty. "You've canceled on me twice now for golf. The least you can do is have lunch with us."

I asked, "Are we talking business?"

"No! It's Sunday," he said, as if indignant that I would suggest it. "This is for catching up on all your adventures."

Audrey didn't look exactly pleased, but nodded her permission, nonetheless.

Simone tugged on my hand. "Can I color on the table?"

* * *

Once in the van, Audrey demanded, "You talk about me with your clients?"

"Just George."

"Why do you need to tell him about me?" she asked with an attitude.

"George and I were supposed to play golf the day you moved in. When I called to cancel, I felt I owed him an explanation. Since then, he's been fascinated by the whole concept of us. Every time I talk with him, he presses for an update."

"Did you tell him I was in jail?"

I hesitated while deciding how best to answer, which itself indicated the answer.

"You did, didn't you?" she said, less as a question and more as a statement. "Why? Why do strangers need to know my business?"

The answer I was searching for finally came to me. "It's endearing," I said.

I felt her eyes boring holes into my neck.

"I'm sorry," I said. "I didn't mean to embarrass you. I never expected you and George to meet."

"So, that makes it okay to use me as a joke?"

"You're not a joke, and George knows that. He and I talk about our lives the way you and other mothers talk about your kids."

I put the van in gear and eased out of the parking space. "You're not a joke," I repeated quietly.

* * *

George was laughing when we met them at the restaurant. "What is that monstrosity you drove up in?" he asked.

Audrey said, "That was Joe's gift to me."

"And you already wrecked it?" George asked.

"Apparently, it came that way," she said.

"It was a gift from her mom *and* me, and it does the job," I defended.

Still laughing, George asked, "What's the job? Scaring other drivers?"

Fortunately, the hostess interrupted George's fun to lead us to our table.

As we walked, Colton came to my defense. "We put the Halloween stickers on it."

"You didn't put 'em on. I did," Simone corrected.

Colton and Royce both rolled their eyes. I didn't know a five-year-old could do that.

The stickers weren't all that scary. Even the ghosts looked friendly. But I don't think George was referring to the stickers.

CHAPTER 48

Audrey

The restaurant had butcher paper and crayons on every table, which was already a win for the kids, but the real showstopper was the antique-style carousel in the middle of the dining room. The kind you'd see at a traveling carnival – fiberglass horses bobbing up and down like they were trying to escape their poles. I'd already promised the kids they could ride after we ordered. I wasn't about to let them eat *first* and then go spin in circles. I assumed management had thought this through, but honestly, who knows.

For now, the kids were busy creating Crayola masterpieces on the butcher paper. The staff had pushed two tables together, and Joe and I sat on either side of the seam like divorced parents at a parent-teacher conference. Simone sat on my right, Colton on Joe's left, and Royce reluctantly took the seat across from Joe and next to George, only after George assured him he didn't bite. Royce looked unconvinced.

After a quick skim of the menu, George launched into his origin story. "I've known Joe for several years, back when he was still a staff accountant. I found out he played golf and had him join me for a round at the country club."

"Matt said my career depended on it," Joe said. "You hadn't been CFO very long at Compassion back then."

Matt was Joe's boss. Apparently golf is the corporate version of hazing.

"But I was with the company long before that," George said. "Back when we were still called Ashtonville Funeral." He nodded toward his wife. "We both were."

That made me sit up. "Did you say *funeral?*"

"Compassion Services is the largest funeral service company in the South," George said proudly, like he was announcing he'd won a chili cook-off.

Joe looked way too amused at my surprise. This felt like something he should've mentioned before we sat down to lunch.

"You know what they say," George continued. "Nothing is certain but death and taxes. My company handles the death, Joe's handles the taxes."

I wondered how many times he'd used that line. Probably enough that Trish could lip-sync it.

After the waitress took our orders, I took the kids to the carousel as promised. When we got back, Trish had taken off her jacket, revealing full sleeve tattoos. Flowers, vines, tigers, dragons, the whole National Geographic special in technicolor. Meanwhile, George had pushed up his sleeves to reveal… absolutely nothing. Just pale, unadorned skin. He looked like a before-picture standing next to her after-picture. And honestly, the contrast between them was the most entertaining thing in the room.

He was mid-story, gesturing with the enthusiasm of a man who had never once ridden a carousel horse in his life.

"So, there we were at the auto parts store," he said. "I handed her my credit card and told her I'd wait in the car. If she's old enough to drive, she's old enough to maintain the car."

Trish leaned forward to catch me up on the story. "He's talking about my daughter. He sent her to the store to buy blinker fluid."

My dad handled all the car maintenance during my youth, but even I knew blinker fluid wasn't a thing.

"A few minutes later, she came out with something in her hand," George said. "I expected her to look mad or embarrassed. But no, she just smiled, got in the car, and handed me a little bottle."

Trish looked at me with a sly smile.

"Then she asked, 'Did I get the right kind?' As if there are different kinds! So, I looked at the bottle, and it said, in large letters across the label, Blinker Fluid.

"She said, 'I got the store brand. It was two dollars cheaper than the name brand.'"

Joe laughed at George's description of the interaction, as Trish smiled at the story she'd heard before.

George continued, "I said, 'Give me that receipt!' I marched up to the store, and as soon as I opened the door, the whole place burst out laughing. Workers, customers, everyone!"

Joe laughed harder, and Trish and I couldn't help but join them. My poor kids had no idea what was so funny.

In a softer voice, George said, "I just turned around and slunk back to the car with my tail between my legs. I told Cassidy she got the right kind."

Joe laughed so hard, he teared up.

"That prank cost me $3.99 plus tax."

Trish grinned and said, "Cassidy keeps that bottle on her dresser like a trophy."

"How many kids do you have?" I asked.

"Four," she answered. "I brought two into the marriage: Cassidy, who's a junior in high school – she's having lunch with friends right now – and Garrett, who's in the army. George also has two. They'd already moved out by the time I came along, but I still count them."

George picked up the conversation. "Preston is my oldest. He's an aerospace engineer for a NASA contractor. Married and has a toddler and a nine-month-old. He lives in Clear Lake. Hunter is a finance guy at one of the energy companies. He and his wife have an apartment near here."

George shook his head and looked down at the table. "I'd hoped they would follow me in the business, but they weren't interested."

I caught Trish rolling her eyes just as George said, "They think it's a dying industry."

I came expecting stuffy executive business talk, but George and Trish both seemed down-to-earth. They didn't look like they'd go together. Yet, they seemed oddly compatible. I liked them.

* * *

I came back from taking Simone to the restroom just in time to hear Joe say, "Here they come."

"Were y'all talking about me?" I joked.

"Audrey," George said, "we only talk about you during our business meetings."

Trish elbowed him so hard he nearly swallowed his tongue.

Colton, blissfully unaware of adult sarcasm, asked, "Can we go on the carousel again?" He asked Joe. Not me. Apparently I'd been demoted.

"Me, too!" Simone added, like she was afraid the carousel might leave without her.

"Not me," Royce said. "That's for little kids."

I hadn't seen a single child projectile-vomit off a fiberglass horse, so I said, "I'll take them."

"No," Joe said, and then turned to Royce with his Dad Voice. "Buddy, I know you think it's for little kids, but you're old enough to help your brother and sister. You're the big brother, so I'm putting you in charge. Help them get on the carousel."

Royce puffed up like a tiny general receiving his first command. "Come on," he said, leading Colton and Simone between the tables with the confidence of someone who had never once lost a sibling in public.

Joe leaned toward me. "The carousel operator won't let them get in trouble."

I watched them get in line behind a mom with two kids, and then saw Royce talking to the ride operator like he was negotiating international policy. My little man had it under control.

George pulled my attention back to the table. "Audrey, this guy was so boring until you came along. That first meeting after you moved in, we spent half the time squeezing as much information out of Joe as we could about the new living arrangement. He's a brave man."

"Or just crazy," Joe said, winking at me.

So Joe tells George and whoever else is in those meetings about my life… then George tells Trish… and Trish probably tells her book club… and her book club probably tells the cashier at the grocery store.

Let's see – BIA parents, the kids' teachers, our Sunday School class, the kids' Sunday School classes, the parents at the bus stop… Honestly, at this point I might as well start a reality show and get paid for the privilege of being everyone's favorite topic.

George chuckled. "Since then, I make him start our calls with the Insta-Fam report."

"Insta-fam?" I asked.

"Instant family. Insta-fam," Trish explained.

George said, "Maybe I should trademark that."

I took a deep breath. "Then I guess he told you where I've been the last few weeks."

Trish put her hand on mine. "We each have our own stories, but I get it. I've been inside, too."

"Jail?" I asked.

She nodded. "Burnet, thirty months. Drugs. Fighting with the cops. I spent my twenties drunk or high or both. My parents practically raised my two kids. But incarceration was the best thing that happened to me. Well, besides George. It stopped my downward spiral and forced me to get sober."

"What about your boys' father?" I asked.

"Dead. Motorcycle accident while I was in jail. Some think it was suicide. I don't know. Anyway, I was out and eventually got a job. Ashtonville was one of the few companies willing to hire an ex-con."

Joe asked what I'd been thinking. "What did you do there?"

"Prepared bodies for burial."

I cringed at the thought of touching dead bodies every day. "Then you met George," I pointed out, eager to imagine an end to the awful job.

"That was a while after I started. I met him a couple of times when I was still at the funeral home. But we really didn't talk until I moved to procurement at corporate."

"I saw her in the hallway now and then," George said. "She was easy to recognize. She put on this tough, aloof façade. I'd say hi, she'd just nod. We really didn't connect until we ended up on the same service project."

Trish smiled broadly. "I didn't think he knew me. He was management and I was just a worker bee. But when our group met up at the project, he greeted me by name."

"Was that at one of the crisis pregnancy centers?" Joe asked.

"Yeah," George said. "We were supposed to paint a couple of rooms and install new shelves."

I was confused. "What does a funeral business have to do with crisis pregnancy centers?"

"Nothing," Trish said. "That's the point. We deal with death and grieving families so much that we get excited about helping new lives. At least, helping others to help others with new lives."

I pictured a firefly landing on a woman's tummy and a soul transferred to the baby inside her.

"We're not there to talk to the clients," George explained. "They have trained counselors for that."

I tried to guess the end of the story. "So, you bonded over painting and fell in love."

I imagined a scene common in so many cheap romcom movies. The lovers paint a room, one accidentally gets paint on the other, then they both sling paint at each other, laughing. Then the lovers have a misunderstanding and get mad at each other, only to later.... Oops. Sometimes my mind runs off on irrelevant tangents.

George and Trish both laughed. "Not quite," he said. "A young woman showed up at the center, a client. That's what they called the women looking for assistance."

"But the counselors were busy with others," Trish said. "So, the woman at the front desk told the girl to take a seat. She did, but she kept looking around and shifting in her chair. Then she got up and left."

George picked up the story. "We're not supposed to interact with the clients, but as soon as she walked out that door, Trish went after her."

"I figured if she left, she wasn't a client anymore," Trish explained.

"I watched their conversation through the glass door," George said. "The girl nodded several times and eventually broke down in tears. I'm thinking, Uh oh, Trish screwed up. But then they hugged and came back in holding hands."

Joe asked, "How did you get her to come back?"

"I just asked her to tell me her story. We connected," Trish said. "Some of the staff at the center that day looked a little too middle-class, if you know what I mean. I think she saw me as someone from her world. And I recognized some of myself in her story. I'd been in her place. Garrett wasn't my first pregnancy. And I've lived with regret over my decision ever since. I didn't judge her but told her we – and I – would support her. I even gave her my number."

"Which was against the rules," George pointed out.

"Screw the rules," Trish said.

"Trish looked like someone who'd pick fights at a biker bar. Watching her talk to that girl showed a tenderness that, to me, seemed out of character."

"I'm not a stereotype," Trish said.

Trish's comment is what I sometimes wanted to tell the world.

George continued, "That episode piqued my interest, and I wanted to know her better. I just didn't know how to do it. I figured I was a little too plain vanilla for her, didn't think she'd be interested. So, I regressed to my awkward teenage years and found excuses to walk by her desk. She had pictures of her kids on her desk, so I'd ask about them. Even brought her coffee a couple of times."

Just then, Simone shouted from across the restaurant, "I'm not a baby!"

Joe put his hand on my arm and said, "I've got this."

George turned to watch him fast-walk toward the carousel, then turned to me and raised his eyebrows. "Wow! He's turned into a real family man."

I had to admit he'd come a long way since we first moved in with him. I guess when I wasn't around, he really had to step up. I'm just surprised he didn't expect me to handle it now that I was back.

I smiled and nodded at George's comment. "Yeah, I guess he has. But back to your story. You brought Trish coffee and worked your way up to asking her out?"

Trish looked at George with a grin and then looked back at me. "I finally got tired of him pussy-footing around and surprised *him* with a coffee. The good kind from the shop next to our building, not the cheap stuff he brought me from the office coffee bar.

George patted her hand. "She'd written her number on the cup."

I couldn't help but smile at the image.

"You're lucky to have Joe," Trish said. "And a lot earlier in life than when I found George."

"I am lucky," I said. "But he sees me as a sister. While I was away, he started seeing someone. Lina."

"I talked to him twice in the last couple of weeks," George said. "He never mentioned Lina. Just you."

I sighed. "She's more his type. No ink. Works for a law firm."

Trish gave me the look of a disappointed mother. "Did you not just hear our story?"

George pointed his finger in my direction. "A wise man once said, 'Where your treasure is, your heart will be also.' From what I've heard so far, Joe's been putting his treasure in you."

Trish pulled his arm down as she focused on me. "Men need respect and appreciation. Give him that, and he'll come around."

"That and coffee," George said.

CHAPTER 49

Joe

The kids and I got back to the table with Audrey in mid-story.

"It still fit all of us, including our parents!" she said.

"Even with seats missing?" Trish asked.

"Yes. That thing is huge. The extra seats are in the garage. 'In case we need to put them back in,' he said. As if eleven seats wouldn't be enough."

The 'he' must be me. "They're in two pairs," I explained. "We could put the left pair back in and still have access to the center aisle. But having both pairs out leaves more room for camping gear."

Audrey looked at me and said, "George said I should put a sign on the van that says, 'Urban Assault Vehicle.' I'm thinking about it."

"Only if you let me paint blast marks on the damaged side," I joked. Actually, I'd been toying with the idea of some kind of humorous décor to embrace the van's faults, such as a picture of Wile E. Coyote flattened against the side in a failed attempt to blow up the Road Runner.

George slapped the table. "Do it! Please! And send me pictures."

Audrey gave me a sly smile and said, "Maybe one day you'll come home from work, and it'll already be done."

Royce's eyes widened. "Momma, that would be so cool!"

I smiled, not just for the potential van art but at the seeming camaraderie of Audrey, George, and Trish. "It sounds like y'all are getting along well without me."

"We're BFFs now," Trish chuckled. "Sharing our deepest secrets."

"I told them about the waitress at Frida's Fajitas," Audrey said. "The look on her face after you-know-who spilled my secret."

She opened her eyes as wide as they would go and stared at Trish with her mouth partly open.

Trish laughed and looked at me to say, "She's hilarious! She already told the story, and I'm still laughing."

* * *

As the kids climbed into the back of the van, Trish hugged me and said, "We should do this again."

She moved on to Audrey, and George slapped my back and said, "You should have introduced us weeks ago. She's a treasure."

On the way home, Audrey surprised me with, "Trish offered me a job. Well, sort of. She suggested it to George, and he agreed."

"Seriously? A job?"

"Yeah. Don't look so surprised," she said.

I recalled what Trish said of her own career. "Preparing dead bodies?"

"Eww! No. Phone work or online chats with potential customers. Sometimes when someone's relative dies, they have no idea what to do. They call or start a chat session through a website with lots of questions. My job would be a little bit of a grief counselor and a little bit of a guide to a local funeral home and the services they have to offer. Trish said I could start with just an hour to two a day. The pay's not great, but I can do it from home. She got me thinking, if it's tolerable, then when Simone starts kindergarten, I could increase my hours."

"Sounds depressing," I said.

"George said to think of it as giving a cup of cold water to a thirsty soul. Anyway, it's money, and I can do it from home."

I understood her points, but it still didn't sound appealing to me.

"Hey," she said. "It still beats handling dead bodies."

After a few seconds of silence, she said, "I'm going to call them. This may be one of the few chances for someone like me to find decent work."

CHAPTER 50

Audrey

After we saw the boys off to school, Simone asked, "Mommy, is Joma ever coming back?"

"Ever?" I said. "You make it sound like she's been gone since the dinosaurs."

"It's been so long," she whined.

It had been *six days*. But kid-time runs on dog-years. "Do you miss her?"

"Yeah."

"Well, let's go visit her."

It felt amazing to have wheels again, even if the van looked like it had survived a small war and then been politely asked to leave. Still better than Dimitri's minivan, which sounded like it was powered by angry crickets. At least this one didn't tick, and the tires weren't bald enough to qualify as a safety hazard.

Before jail, I used to fill the gaps between chores with long, pointless walks around the neighborhood. Now I could run errands like a normal person – or, you know, stalk family members on a whim.

We drove to Joanna's house, but she wasn't home. I probably should've called first, but I have no idea what child-free housewives do all day. I just assumed she'd be home, sipping tea and alphabetizing her pantry.

Instead, she answered through the doorbell speaker like we were suspicious solicitors. She'd gone shopping and would be back in an hour.

Simone looked crushed as she climbed from my driver's seat to her actual seat.

"Let's go see Nana's old house," I said.

Mom had already moved out and was staying with Uncle Johnny until her new house arrived – literally arrived like a giant Amazon package – in two weeks. Since we were nearby, I wanted one last look at the place where I grew up.

The For Sale sign was gone, but the driveway was empty, and the leaves on the sidewalk suggested the new owners had not yet embraced their landscaping responsibilities. Simone unbuckled herself before I even stopped the car.

The second I opened my door, she wedged herself between the front seats like a tiny escape artist and bolted to the front door. She pressed her face to its window.

"There's nothing inside," she said.

Oof. I felt that one in my bones.

I looked past her into the empty house. No furniture. No pictures. No future – not for us, anyway. Mom probably had photos somewhere, either in an album or on a flash drive she'd never find again.

But the house was more than stuff. It was Christmases and Thanksgivings and birthdays. Easter egg hunts in the backyard. Ballet pirouettes on the living room floor. And my first kiss with Joe right there at that front door.

"Mommy?"

"Yeah, baby?"

"You look sad."

"No, baby," I lied. "I'm just thinking about what it used to look like when I lived here."

Apparently, nostalgia wasn't contagious.

"Can we get French fries before we go home?"

"Sure. That sounds good."

Home. What did that even mean anymore?

* * *

French fries meant a trip to McDonald's—the fancy kind with a playground, where the fries are hot, the ketchup is free, and the germs build character. We got back with plenty of time before the boys would be home.

There it was again. *Home.*

Somewhere deep inside, I still thought of Mom's house as "back home," as in, when things in Beaumont got bad, I moved "back home." But I didn't have a "back home" anymore. It had been boxed up, sold off, and probably Febreze'd by strangers.

So… was *this* it now? Joe's house? The place where Simone and the boys would someday say, "Remember when we were little and lived there?"

"She did the workbooks with me," Simone said.

"What?" I asked, realizing I hadn't been paying attention.

"When Joma was here, she did the workbooks with me."

"What workbooks?" I asked.

She went to the cabinet under the waterless wet bar by the door to the back yard and pulled out a stack of paperback books the size of magazines. "These workbooks."

Reading. Writing. Shapes. Numbers. Even beginner readers.

"Joma was teaching you to read?" I asked

"Mm hmm," she confirmed. She ran back to the cabinet and pulled out a hardcover book. "I can read this one."

Green Eggs and Ham by Dr. Seuss.

"Are you telling me that in one month, Joma taught you to read?"

"Not Royce's books. But I can read this one."

She plopped herself onto the sofa, with her little legs sticking straight out in front of her, and opened the book in her lap. As she proceeded to read the simple, one-syllable words of the story, I sat beside her and listened. She touched each word with a finger as she said it.

Her ability was impressive. When she finished, I asked, "Did you really read it or just memorize it?"

She opened the book again and pointed to a word in the middle of the page.

"Fox," she said. Then she pointed to another word and said, "This one's 'would.' It tries to trick you 'cause the L doesn't make a sound."

"I agree it's tricky," I told her, still amazed she knew it.

"That's what Joma said. Tricky."

I knew Joe's mother painted the living room and bedrooms, but I didn't know what else she did to keep Simone occupied. I suddenly realized I needed to show my appreciation to those who cared for my kids when I couldn't.

While Simone practiced her letters in one of Joanna's workbooks, I got out my phone and searched for florists.

"Holy *Spitzbergen!*"

It cost $70 to have flowers delivered, and that was the cheapest option. A dozen roses in a vase with baby's breath were easily over $100. Two dozen during February must cost a fortune. No wonder no one ever sent me roses. My bank account didn't have much more than that in it. I've hardly touched the account since living with Joe, since he pays for groceries and household supplies. But every month, the bank deducts a few dollars from my account for the privilege of keeping my money in their bank. They don't charge that to the rich people, only the poor ones like me.

I forgot to call Trish! The noisy rumbling of a school bus somewhere in the neighborhood prompted me to check the time. The boys would be home any minute, dashing any chance for a private phone call with a potential employer. I taped a reminder to my bathroom mirror just as Simone yelled, "The bus is here!"

* * *

The next morning, I called Trish about the funeral home job. If she could handle dead bodies, I could at least handle talking to their loved ones about funeral arrangements.

"I'll text you a link to the job description," Trish said, wrapping up the call. "It's pretty detailed."

"You're sure they'd let me do it even if I only have a couple of hours a day?" I asked.

"It's not ideal," she said, "but we'd consider it a training period. Check out the listing on the website, and if you're still interested, I'll arrange a visit to one of our affiliates."

"Affiliates?"

"One of the funeral homes. See firsthand how they do things."

"Okay. Is that where they teach me all the funeral home jokes?"

Trish laughed. "I learned most of them from George after I moved to corporate." She turned serious again when she said, "The business isn't as bad as people think."

We ended the call, and I checked the time.

"Come on, monkey," I said to Simone. "We're going shopping."

We drove to a thrift store run by a Christian charity. I bought the only two vases they had for three dollars each. I would have bought another if they had one. I may have to pay another visit in a few days. Our next stop was the supermarket for flowers and Thank You cards.

CHAPTER 51

Joe

Debbie appeared in the doorway of my office holding a vase of assorted flowers.

"I found these at the reception desk," she said.

"Oh? You have an admirer?" I asked, curious as to why she thought to personally show me.

She set the vase down on my desk. "No. You do," she said, holding up an envelope with my name on it. Then she handed it to me with an amused smile.

She left before I opened the envelope.

For the next two hours, passersby stopped in to ask who the flowers were from. Upon learning they were from Audrey, the women said, "Aww," in that sing-song tone they use when seeing a baby.

The guys turned it into a whole word, as in, "That's awesome!"

"No girl's ever gotten me flowers," a male senior manager said.

"Not even my wife," a partner lamented.

"That's why it's awesome," a senior associate said.

Debbie caught me carrying the flowers on my way out that evening and stopped me. I sometimes go days without seeing her, and today I encountered her twice.

"You knew they were from Audrey, didn't you?" I asked.

She grinned. "Lucy described the woman who dropped them off. Not many women have a lotus tattoo on their neck. And she had a little girl with her."

She reached for the vase, and I let her take it rather than risk dropping it in a tug-of-war.

"Joe, she could have had those waiting for you at home," she said. "She sent them here for a reason. Leave them here; she wants others to know she cares about you."

That caught me off guard. The card didn't mention anything about love, romance, or caring, other than the "Love Audrey" signature.

"Um, it was a … It was a Thank You card," I stammered. "She was thanking me for helping her and taking care of the kids."

Debbie didn't acknowledge my response. She just said, "I'll put them back in your office," as she turned toward the inner hallway.

As I walked to my car parked two blocks away in a cheap surface lot, a shabbily dressed street preacher standing on the low wall of a flowerbed in front of an office building paused his message and pointed at me. He had a circuit of different blocks to preach his sermons each day and alternated between messages of doom and God's love for mankind. I'd long since tuned him out.

I only caught him in mid-sentence when he pointed directly at me as I passed. "…His love," he barked.

"What?" I asked, startled by the gesture that invaded my personal space.

"God has an audacious love. A love of forgiveness and second chances. And third and fourth."

He then turned toward others walking by and shouted his message of, "Repent and accept his love because you won't like the alternative!"

Audacious. I used to tease Audrey with that term back in high school. Audacious Audrey. I even compressed it into an adjective to use whenever she had a notable idea: Audracious, with an "R." Ironically, she was not an audacious person back then when I used the term far too often for less-than-notable ideas. It seemed like her audacious side came out after she dumped me for Europe.

Seated in my car, I pulled out her card and read it again.

Thank you for taking care of the kids
and me when you didn't have to.
Thank you for visiting me in jail.
Thank you for giving us a home.

Love, Audrey.

It was audacious for a woman to send flowers to a man.

CHAPTER 52

Audrey

Simone dropped her pencil like it had personally offended her and shouted, "Joe!" the second he walked in the back door.

I stood at the sink, scrubbing the pan I'd used for dinner, trying to look domestic instead of exhausted. Joe held up my Thank You card as if displaying evidence in court.

Simone bounced in place. "Did you like the flowers?"

"I did," he said. "The whole office was jealous."

Simone lit up like she'd just won Employee of the Month.

I kept scrubbing, waiting for him to say something else. After a few seconds of silence, I glanced over. He was still standing there, staring at me with a tiny smile like he'd forgotten what words were.

I smiled back. "What?"

"Barefoot and in the kitchen," he said.

I looked down. Yes, my feet were bare. But I was wearing sweatpants and a hoodie I'd stolen from his closet, not exactly a 1950s housewife fantasy. I shrugged.

"Isn't that the way men want us?" I asked, smirking.

"Maybe once upon a time," he said, dropping his computer bag in a chair and walking toward me.

He placed a hand on the small of my back and started rubbing slow circles as if trying to hypnotize me.

"The flowers were *audracious*,"he said. "Thank you."

I couldn't help smiling at my old high-school nickname turned adjective. No one had used it in years. I dropped the sponge and grabbed a dish towel to dry my hands.

"You're not supposed to thank me for thanking you," I said.

His hand slid from my back to my side, and he pulled me into a warm, sideways hug.

I turned to face him. "I just wanted you to know I appreciate you." I gave him a quick squeeze before stepping away and calling, "Kids, dinner's ready! Remember, tonight's BIA night."

Because nothing kills a tender moment faster than reminding everyone we have somewhere to be.

* * *

With only moderate urging, Colton headed off for his bath as soon as we returned from the meeting. Royce worked at the kitchen table, filling in vocabulary blanks with the seriousness of a tiny scholar. Simone colored in her book, humming with the confidence of an artist who never doubts her own genius.

With all three children occupied, granting me a rare few minutes before Simone's bath, I stretched out on the sofa. Joe usually disappeared to his bedroom desk at this point, but tonight he walked over, lifted my legs, and sat exactly where my feet had been. My bare feet ended up in his lap, which felt both surprising and suspiciously intentional.

"Your feet are cold," he said.

"You can warm them up for me," I teased.

"You want me to touch your stinky feet?"

"Too late. You already did," I said, wiggling my toes for emphasis.

He rubbed my ankles and the tops of my feet. I couldn't tell whether he was trying to warm them through friction or attempting some amateur reflexology.

That reminded me of my conversation with Mom earlier. "Mom wants to take me for a massage on Saturday," I told him. "And then to get our nails done."

"Girls' day, eh?" he said, placing one hand on the sole of my left foot and the other on top.

"What are you doing?" I asked. "Creating a hand sandwich? Or is this a foot sandwich?"

"You're so funny," he said.

Then he brushed his hand across my sole, and I jerked my feet back in a full-body tickle spasm. "Don't!" I squealed.

Simone and Royce both looked up, startled by the sudden chaos.

Joe pulled his hands back and grinned. "Mommy's ticklish."

Before I could protest, he wrapped one arm around both my ankles, pinning my feet to his chest, and launched a full assault with his free hand. I dissolved into helpless laughter, thrashing until I slid off the sofa and landed on the floor in a heap.

As I lay there panting, Simone ran to Joe and shouted, "Do me! Do me!"

Royce groaned. "You're too noisy. I'm trying to do vocabulary."

I stayed on the floor, watching Joe pull Simone onto his lap and then listening to her giggles fill the room as he tickled her ribs.

Moments like this made me wish every evening could unfold with this much joy.

CHAPTER 53

Joe

Last night, after the kids had gone to bed, I found Audrey sitting on the sofa and staring expressionlessly at the fireplace. It had no fire in it. Not even a log. Contemplation wasn't a typical Audrey behavior.

I asked, "What are you thinking about?

She merely shrugged and said, "Life and other stuff."

"Life's a rather broad topic," I pointed out. "I can't imagine what other stuff wouldn't fall under the life category."

She looked up and me and said, "Gravity and the physics of falling objects." She didn't give so much as a smile. Then she went back to staring at the logless fireplace. I'm pretty sure that wasn't what she was thinking. That was the end of that conversation.

Today was different. I don't know what prompted her to send flowers, but whatever it was must have helped her get over the funk she was in. I almost didn't attempt to bother her on the sofa. But given that she gave me flowers and had a more cheerful demeanor in the kitchen, I took a chance. When I put her feet in my lap, I half expected her to pull them away from me and sit up. But she didn't. I caught a glimpse of high-school Audrey in that interaction.

When she got out of the shower, I told her, "Keep Friday night open. I want to take you out to dinner. Steaks. Just us, not the kids."

"What about Lina?" she asked.

Why would she bring up Lina?

"I didn't know you two were that close," I said. "I thought it would be just the two of us, but I can invite her if you want."

"No, no. Just us is fine," she assured.

"Okay, good. I already texted your mom," I said. "She can come over and watch the kids."

CHAPTER 54

Audrey

Friday night marked my first kid-free outing in ages. *Fun* kid-free, not "court date" kid-free. I even wore a dress and lipstick, which felt borderline ceremonial. Mom took the kids to one of those chaotic pizza-arcade-bowling hybrids where children go to lose their minds and adults go to lose their will to live.

"Do you see these prices?" I whispered, holding up the menu as if it were a sacred text.

Bryant's Steakhouse was the kind of place I used to dream of working at – where a single entrée cost as much as two meals, an appetizer, and drinks at my old job. I could've paid rent with three nights of tips here. Maybe two if I smiled.

Joe chuckled. "I've been here before."

"Dad used to take us to places like this," I said. "Back when… well, before the shop closed. But only twice a year. Maximum."

Joe nodded. "Definitely not an everyday thing. What are you having?"

"Still deciding. What made you want to go out tonight?"

He shrugged. "It's been a while since I've been on a date. Figured it's been a while for you, too."

A date. He said it so casually, as if he hadn't spent years dodging my flirtations with the agility of a ninja. But if he wanted to call this a date, I wasn't about to argue.

I'd gone on a couple of dates earlier in the year, both with customers from the restaurant. Things fizzled the moment they learned I had three kids. Before that, I hadn't been with anyone since my last boyfriend moved out of our Beaumont apartment two years ago. The romance evaporated the moment he moved in, and he eventually found a woman who didn't come with bonus children. I just wish he'd moved out before I discovered her existence.

None of those men opened the car door for me the way Joe did tonight. The way he used to in high school.

When I ordered a grilled chicken salad, Joe clicked his tongue and told the waiter, "Scratch that. She's having the filet mignon."

The waiter looked at me. I looked at Joe. Joe nodded. I surrendered.

"Yeah," I said. "The filet mignon."

Over wine and steak, we talked about my spa day with Mom tomorrow, his golf outing with George, and Simone's upcoming birthday party.

"I talked to Trish about that phone job," I said.

Joe made a face that suggested he'd bitten into a lemon. "The one where you make funeral arrangements?"

"Yep. She said I can take the training course first and decide after."

"When was this?"

I thought back. "Tuesday."

"And the next day George called to invite me to golf tomorrow," he said slowly.

I grinned. "You're welcome."

He blinked, processing the idea that I had done something beneficial for him. "Thank you," he finally said. Then, "Okay, since George invited me and you're spending the day with your mom, who's watching the kids?"

"Already handled. Livvy's mom invited Royce to the zoo. And Mom convinced Liam and Cami to watch Colton and Simone. The spa's near their neighborhood, so I'll drop them off first."

"I think Livvy has a thing for Royce," he said.

"Mom said she's been coming over a lot."

"Maybe she wants to play doctor," Joe said with a smirk.

"Joe! They're eight!"

"I'm just saying – he patched her up after she fell. Doctor stuff. But maybe you should give him the sex talk." He paused, then added, "No, wait. With your track record, maybe *I* should give him the sex talk."

My jaw dropped. "You did NOT go there!"

He grinned, daring me to deny it. I couldn't.

"Come on," he coaxed. "Admit that was funny."

It *was* funny – from anyone else's perspective. But I refused to give him the satisfaction. I crossed my wrists on the table, crossed my legs under it, and glared with all the dignity of a woman who had just been roasted by her date.

Then something bumped my dangling foot hard enough to knock my shoe off. Joe's grin widened. He snorted.

I snorted back.

The waiter returned for Joe's credit card, placing the bill inside a little black leather portfolio as if it contained state secrets. At my old restaurant, we used a plastic tray that cracked if you breathed on it.

Joe checked the time. "We've still got a couple hours before your mom turns into a pumpkin."

"Oh yeah?"

"I'm thinking we hit the Triple S."

"The what?"

"Strait Shot Saloon."

"A bar, huh?" I raised my glass in a mock toast and finished the wine. "You just want to get me drunk so you can have your way with me."

He snorted. "Yeah, something like that. I'm driving, so I'll stick to something non-alcoholic. But you go right ahead. Just know that if you get too drunk to walk, I'll throw you over my shoulder and carry you out like a rolled-up carpet."

And honestly? That sounded fantastic.

CHAPTER 55

Joe

The Strait Shot Saloon was old school. Neon beer signs behind the long oak bar and tables with red and white checkered tablecloths arranged around a dance floor. The country band covered songs released long before I was born, and the music on the antique-style jukebox, which was locked down while the band played, appeared to be from a time capsule buried in 1995. The place opened about ten years ago yet looked like it's been around fifty.

Out on the dance floor, I held Audrey's right hand in my left, my other hand on her waist, hers on my shoulder. At the third song, I realized this was the longest we'd touched each other in years. I looked down at her, and she smiled.

She leaned in to tell me, "I haven't done this kind of dancing since prom."

I can't say I've been dancing a lot, but I've been a few times since college, usually with a group of guys and girls. Once on a double date.

"You didn't go clubbing in Europe?" I asked.

"Yeah, but I didn't hear any country music."

We were both too rusty for our spins to look as smooth as those of other couples. When the band announced a break, Audrey looked at me with pouty lips.

"Get that table before someone else nabs it," I said, pointing to a vacant table. "I'll go get drinks. You want a double shot of tequila, right?"

She tilted her head and scowled at me. "Margarita. Regular, not double."

At the bar, I felt a hand on my back. Not just a light touch but a full pat. I turned to find Lina standing behind me.

"Hey, Joe!" she said, grinning.

"Lina! How long have you been here?"

"We got here just before the band took a break," she said. "I saw you and Audrey on the dance floor."

Another woman put her hand on Lina's shoulder and smiled at me. "Hi."

Lina glanced at her and then back at me. "This is Erin, we work together." Then, to her, she said, "This is Joe. Our kids are in Boys in Action together. He's the one I told you about."

The whole "our kids" thing has become so common now that I just roll with it. No one wants to pause a conversation while I explain the relationship.

"Oh," Erin said. She gave me a sly smile while saying to Lina, "The one you shared the tent with."

I laughed and said to Lina, "You're supposed to stop the rumors, not spread them."

She shrugged and tilted her chin up defiantly. "Life needs more spice."

"Girls' night out?" I asked.

"Not quite," Lina said. "Our guys are around here somewhere."

Erin tilted her head toward the far end of the bar. "Mine's over there getting drinks."

"And mine was parking the car," Lina said.

"Grant?" I asked.

She wrinkled her forehead. "No. Grant's just a friend. I'm here with Lance."

Erin explained, "He's in-house counsel for one of her firm's clients."

"Ah," I said. "I've heard the dance floor is a great place to discuss legal strategy."

She waved a finger up in front of my face. "If that's how he wants to spend his time with me, I'll catch an Uber home." She and Erin both laughed at that remark.

I returned to the table with Lina, Erin, and Erin's boyfriend, Hunter, in tow.

"Look who I found!" I said.

I thought Audrey would be pleased to see Lina after asking about her a few days ago. However, her demeanor said otherwise. Her smile evaporated when she saw Lina, but she quickly put it on again before saying, "Wow! Lina! Crazy seeing you here!"

CHAPTER 56

Audrey

"Then Lina showed up," I told Mom, who lay on the massage table next to mine, her face smushed into the headrest like a tranquilized pancake.

"Who's Lina?" she asked, her voice muffled.

"Her son's in Royce's BIA crew. She's the one who gave Joe that giant photo of me that's hanging in the living room. She's also pretty, single, and flirts with every single dad in a five-mile radius."

"And with Joe," Mom said. "That's what's really bothering you."

I groaned as the masseuse pressed into a knot that apparently held all my unresolved issues. "I may have embarrassed myself."

"What did you do?" Mom asked, already bracing for impact.

"I asked Joe point-blank if he picked that place because he knew Lina would be there."

"You asked in front of Lina?"

"Yep. Full audience. And with attitude." I sighed. "She giggled. Not even a real laugh. A giggle. That made it worse."

"Did he?" Mom asked.

"Did he what?"

"Pick the place because she'd be there."

"They both denied it," I said. "She even said she never talks about her date plans with Joe."

"Date plans?"

"Apparently, she has a boyfriend now. And right after she said that, some older guy showed up and kissed her. I don't know if my jealousy leaked out when I asked, but after that I felt... petty. Very petty."

"Well, you must've made up," Mom said. "Because you were pretty giggly when y'all got home."

Mom didn't know the half of it. She'd passed out on Joe's bed after putting the kids to sleep. Thank goodness she wasn't in the living room when we walked in. When she finally found us, I was lying on the sofa while Joe stood over me with his hands on his hips, looking proud enough to be on a motivational poster.

A few more spins around the dance floor and another margarita had washed away my Lina-related humiliation. By the time we got home, I was feeling good. I mean, really good.

Joe shut off the car and opened his door. I didn't move. Eyes closed, not asleep. Just savoring the moment like a cat in a sunbeam.

"We're home," he said.

He came around to my side and opened the door. I still didn't move.

"Time to get out."

I looked up at him. "I'm too tired to get out." Translation: I'm relaxed and dramatic.

He grabbed my hands and pulled me upright. Instead of walking toward the house, I did my best impression of a fainting Victorian heroine and leaned into him.

"Do I have to carry you?" he asked.

"You promised."

"When did I promise that?"

"When we were leaving the steakhouse."

He snorted. "That wasn't a promise. It was a threat."

I remained limp and uncooperative.

In one smooth motion, he crouched, grabbed my legs, and hoisted me over his shoulder. Exactly the rolled-up-carpet maneuver he'd warned me about. He carried me to the back door while I giggled the entire way.

It's a miracle the kids didn't wake up.

A sharp press from the masseuse snapped me back to the present. I hadn't realized my muscles were auditioning for a concrete sculpture exhibit.

"You like Joe, don't you?" Mom asked.

I exhaled. "Mom. I never stopped liking him. I just didn't think it would ever work out."

"Not even after he invited you to move in?"

"Especially after he let me move in. The whole thing felt half business, half charity. What did I bring to the table besides chaos and expenses?"

"He took you to dinner and dancing last night. That's not nothing, Sweetie."

"Yeah. He's been extra nice since I got back. I just don't know what it means."

What I didn't tell her was the truth: I didn't want to get my hopes up.

"Maybe he finally understands what you deal with as a mom," she said. "A month with your kids would give anyone a spiritual awakening."

CHAPTER 57

Joe

Royce and I met George at the entrance of the restaurant at the Briar Village Golf Course. He leaned against the wall, sipping coffee, with his golf bag next to him.

"I see you brought a caddy," George greeted jovially.

"You remember Royce," I said.

"Hi, Mr. George," Royce said.

"He was supposed to go to the zoo with his girlfriend," I explained. "But her mom texted late last night and said she came down with a fever."

"She's not my girlfriend," Royce complained.

"Oh, sorry," I said. Then I corrected with, "He was going with a *friend* who happens to be a *girl*."

Royce gave me a sour pickle look as if my correction didn't meet his satisfaction.

"And who happens to have a crush on him," I added.

"That's not my fault," Royce defended.

"Well, it sort of is," I pointed out.

George chuckled. "Sounds like I'm already getting the Insta-Fam report."

To Royce, he said, "Glad to have you on board, Royce. I don't see any clubs with you. Are you playing or just caddying?"

"I don't know how to play," he said.

George shot me a look of disappointment. He shook his head and said, "Joe, you'd better tip him well."

"I told him the grill here has the best burgers in town."

"Are you buying?" George asked.

"I'm buying his, not yours," I countered.

George looked at his watch and said, "Let's hit the course. By the way, they've paired us up with a couple of old geezers. A father and son. And the father looks about a hundred years old. Let's just hope he doesn't have a heart attack before the eighteenth hole. Don't want to be interrupted by a medical emergency."

Royce's eyes grew wide at George's comments. "They didn't teach us what to do for a heart attack."

"I think George is kidding," I assured. To George, I explained, "He's been learning first aid with the Boys in Action."

"I'm only half kidding," George said. "And I still want that Insta-fam report."

The report would have to wait until we teed off. We and the pair of elderly gentlemen may technically be a foursome, but other than polite greetings, George, Royce, and I stuck to ourselves.

George drove us in the golf cart to where his ball landed across the fairway. On the way, he turned to look at Royce, sitting behind us, and asked, "Royce, how do you like living with Joe?"

I glanced back at Royce.

"Okay, I guess," he said. "He doesn't cook as good as Momma or Nana."

I squinted at him and asked, "That's what you lead with? That I'm a bad cook?"

I think he took the hint.

"Joe's way better than the guy we used to live with."

According to Audrey, that relationship ended early last year. I wondered if Royce's comment was about cooking or something else. Before I could ask, George beat me to it.

"How's that?" he asked.

"He didn't do anything with us," Royce explained. "He didn't talk to us or take us anywhere. All he did was grab Momma's butt all the time."

George faked concern. "And Joe doesn't grab your momma's butt?"

"Not when I'm around," Royce said.

"Do you think he should?" George asked, winking at me.

Royce scrunched up his face and asked, "Why?" in a tone that also seemed to say, "You're weird."

We paused our chatter to complete the first hole and move on to the second. Despite the advanced age of our partners, they drove their car like they were in a NASCAR race. The younger one, who must have been in his seventies, turned the wheel sharply and skidded to a halt like a stuntman in an action film. I was amazed that the older one didn't fly out of his seat.

George slowed to a stop behind them and asked me, "So, what else happened this week?"

Apparently, Royce was enjoying his role in the Insta-Fam report and thought George was still talking to him. "Momma took flowers to Joe at his work," he said. "I was still at school, but my sister told me when I got home."

George looked at me and asked, "What did you do to deserve that?"

"I don't know," I said. "The card said she was thanking me for basically everything. But I don't know what prompted it on Tuesday."

"That's the day she called Trish about the job," George recalled.

"Yeah, and the next day you called me about golf," I pointed out.

"Trish told me Audrey hinted that you missed golf. And it so happened that my partner canceled on me. He went out of town for a family emergency."

"I'm sorry to hear that. But I'm glad you kept me in mind."

"Well, I'm living vicariously through your stories," he said.

"Are you gonna tell him about last night?" Royce asked me.

George raised his eyebrows and turned to me. "Yeah, Joe, are you going to tell me about last night?"

Now it was getting more personal. "Audrey and I went out to dinner," I admitted.

"Ooh. Just the two of you? No kids?"

"And then they went dancing," Royce added.

"How do you know that?" I asked. We didn't plan that part before we left the house. I mean, I thought about it, but didn't tell Audrey until I saw how dinner went.

"Nana told us," Royce said. "They were laughing when they came back."

I guess my text to Beverly made its way to the kids. I said. "You were supposed to be asleep."

"I was until y'all got home."

I hope he didn't know why we were laughing. Last night, Audrey claimed to be tipsy from the wine at dinner and drinks at the bar. I suspected she was just faking it. Whatever it was, she wanted assistance with getting from the car to the house. So, I did what any gentleman would do. I threw her over my shoulder and carried her in. She wouldn't stop giggling.

Before opening the back door, I slapped her bottom. "Shh. Carpets don't laugh," I scolded, trying to keep from laughing myself.

"Maybe I'm a magic carpet," she said as I carried her through the door.

"A magic carpet, huh? Are you gonna give me a ride?"

She giggled again. "What kind of ride do you have in mind?"

That deserved another slap on her butt. "I walked right into that one, didn't I?" I said with a chuckle.

I carried her past the lighted breakfast area and into the darkened living room. I'd expected Beverly to be waiting for us on the sofa. Seeing it empty, I dumped Audrey there.

She teased, "Is this where you want that ride?"

I grabbed her hands and pulled her to sit up. "As tempting as that sounds, you know my position on sleeping together."

"Lying down?" she asked, still holding onto my hands.

I knew the kids were asleep, but I couldn't help chuckling. I said, "We should be married before that kind of activity."

She responded with, "I accept."

"Accept what?"

"Your proposal. You just said we should be married. I accept."

That caught me off guard. As I tried to think of a witty reply, I heard, "Shh, shh, shh."

We looked up to see Beverly shushing us from the bedroom hallway. When she had our attention, she asked, "Did y'all have fun?"

CHAPTER 58

Audrey

"You're getting Simone a bike for her birthday, right?" I asked Mom as we walked from the massage place to the nail salon, both of us moving with the loose-limbed wobble of people who'd been kneaded into submission.

"Yes, I already have it," she said. "Well, it's at Alan's place. He helped me pick it out."

"Did you know about the training bike?"

"That old thing with the training wheels? Joanna brought it over a couple weeks ago. Apparently Joe asked her to keep an eye out for a used kids' bike. Simone couldn't wait to tell me she was practicing for the new one I'm getting her."

I didn't need to tell her Simone's enthusiasm had only intensified. "She's been riding it up and down the cul-de-sac all week. She made Joe take the training wheels off a few days ago. He didn't stand a chance."

After the massage and nail salon, Mom had her own Big Reveal. I followed her old Lexus RX350 into a manufactured home dealership between Katy and Sealy. Thanksgiving was still weeks away, but the place already looked ready for Santa's annual performance review.

Mom pointed to a tiny beige house with dark trim and a tin roof. "That's the one I bought," she said, practically vibrating. "Well, not that exact one, but that model. They'll deliver it next week."

"Just in time for Thanksgiving," I said.

"I think my days of hosting Thanksgiving are over."

Last year had been my first Thanksgiving with her in ages. Weird to think the tradition had marched on without me. Even weirder to think it wouldn't happen again. That hollow feeling from Monday crept back in, tapping me on the shoulder.

Mom led me up the steps to the porch. It was empty, but I could already picture two rocking chairs and a seasonal wreath that would fall off every time the wind blew. Inside, the dealership had gone full holiday mode. A tiny Christmas tree stood in the corner, and tinsel wrapped around the railings like festive boa constrictors.

"Mom, the house is cute, but your old Christmas tree won't fit."

"I know. I have to downsize everything, even Christmas. For now, all the decorations are in Johnny's barn with the rest of my stuff."

"Can I have the tree?"

"Of course. Take the tree and any ornaments you want. I'll bring them over next week when I come for Simone's birthday."

* * *

When I saw Joe again that afternoon, I asked about his golf game.

He responded, "Good."

At the same time, Royce said, "Boring. And he lost."

"By only two strokes! And in my defense, I haven't gotten to play in a while. It felt good to get on the course again."

"And Mr. George started calling me Rolls Royce," Royce complained.

"I'm sorry you were so miserable," I said. "Next time you can go to Uncle Liam's with Colton and Simone."

"That's okay. I'd rather go with Joe and Mr. George."

Did that mean he wasn't so miserable after all, or that he thought my brother's place would be worse? Colton and Simone didn't seem to mind. Apparently, Cami wasn't that grumpy today.

"George let him drive the golf cart," Joe said.

"Until that worker came and yelled at us," Royce said.

Joe laughed. "He didn't yell, he just told George that kids aren't allowed to drive the carts."

Royce offered a sulky defense of, "Mr. George said I was a good driver."

Joe asked me, "How was your spa day?"

"Good. Relaxing." I paused a millisecond to add, "I invited Mom to have Thanksgiving with us."

"Here?" he asked.

"Yes. Here."

"Do you know how much work that is?"

"She'll help. And I want your parents and Ava to come, too. And Liam's family."

I could see the wheels turning in his head. "Twelve people," he said. "This isn't like a kid's birthday party with pizza."

"Thirteen," I corrected. "Mom wants to bring Dr. Alan."

CHAPTER 59

Joe

Audrey didn't put up any resistance to my suggestion of having Simone's birthday party at the park instead of the house. She invited the kids from Simone's Sunday School class. There weren't as many as at Colton's party, but I don't think Simone noticed.

The theme was unicorns. We had a unicorn piñata, a unicorn cake, and played ring toss on the unicorn's horn. Audrey's mother offered face painting, with an emphasis on unicorns and rainbows.

While the cleanup was easier than with Colton's party at the house, I hadn't counted on the hassle of transporting borrowed chairs and tables and party supplies from home to the park and back home later. Now I understand the appeal of having a birthday party at a place like Chuck E. Cheese or Squirrel Bob's. The only things you have to pack up and haul away are the gifts.

* * *

When I got home Monday night, a fully decorated Christmas tree stood in the living room by the wall between the bedroom hallway and the door to the back porch. Audrey and the kids stood next to it, grinning from ear to ear.

"Isn't it pretty?" Audrey asked.

"Yeah, it's great! But where did it come from?"

We hadn't even talked about Christmas decorations. I could already hear my dad complaining, *It's not even Thanksgiving!*

"Mom brought it over Saturday when she came from the birthday party," she said. "She and Dr. Alan unloaded it into the dining room while we were getting the party stuff ready. It's from our old house."

How did I miss that? Did I not even look in the dining room since then? Oh yeah, Saturday night, we had leftover pizza in front of the TV. Sunday night, she had the kids eat early at the kitchen table, while she and I ate there after them.

"And look at the fireplace," Colton said, pointing.

Four stockings hung there. One with Audrey's name hung on the far left. That was followed by stockings for Royce, Colton, and Simone. They left room for another stocking on the right, after Simone's.

"I'll get a stocking for you next time I go shopping," Audrey assured. Then she asked, "Can we put up lights on the house?"

I thought again of something my dad often said. I parroted his words, "We means me, doesn't it?"

"I'll hold the ladder," Audrey offered.

CHAPTER 60

Audrey

Joe's mother arrived early to help with the cooking, armed with enough Tupperware to supply a small army. Mom and Dr. Alan showed up just before noon, with Joe's dad and his sister Ava right behind them. I barely recognized Ava. No braces, shorter hair, and a whole vibe of "I have my life together," even though she was wearing jeans and a red mock turtleneck. Honestly, the turtleneck might've been doing most of the heavy lifting. My last memory of her was from high school, when she was still in her chrysalis stage.

"I love the decorations!" she said. "Dad always made us wait until after Thanksgiving to put ours up."

"It takes away from Thanksgiving," he grumbled. "People jump straight from Halloween to Christmas with no time to be thankful."

I smiled. "That's how it was at our house, too. But when Mom brought the decorations over, my self-control evaporated."

Liam's family was the last to arrive. My kids were busy giving Ava a tour of the house, probably pointing out all the places they'd spilled things. Meanwhile, Joe, Mr. Steve, and Dr. Alan sat in the living room drinking iced tea and discussing college football with the seriousness of diplomats negotiating a peace treaty.

Mom had just finished setting the table when Liam, Cami, and Hannah walked in.

"Mom, they already have their Christmas tree up," Hannah announced. "Why didn't we put ours up?"

"I don't have as much time as your Aunt Audrey," Cami said. "She doesn't have a job."

Joe overheard that and immediately stood up for me. "Audrey has a job."

"Yeah, well, housework for you isn't full-time," Cami said.

"I'm not talking about the housework," Joe said. "She just got a real job."

I stepped out of the kitchen to clarify. "Well… not yet. I'm doing the online training."

Liam jumped in. "Do they pay you while you're training?"

"No," I admitted. "Not until I start taking calls."

"Calls?" he asked. "You mean those annoying cold calls about insurance or roofing or extended warranties?"

I had the perfect line ready, courtesy of George. "No. Cold calls are for warm bodies. These are warm calls for cold bodies."

Joe snorted. Apparently that was one of George's jokes he hadn't heard yet.

"I'll be answering calls for funeral services," I explained.

Cami tilted her head, doing her best judgmental-owl impression. "Funeral services? So you're exploiting people's grief for profit?"

I took a deep breath. "No. I'll be helping people through their grief. A lot families don't know about making final arrangements. We guide them through the process and handle the details so they can focus on family and memories." Yes, I stole that from a training video. No regrets.

Liam made a harumph noise. "If they're not paying you for the training, it's not a real job."

I ignored both of them and escaped to the garage to get the camping table before I said something that would require a second funeral.

We inserted the extension leaf into the dining table to fit nine adults. That meant six dining chairs and three folding chairs Joe's dad brought from his truck, because apparently he travels with emergency seating. My original plan was to put the kids at the kitchen table, but Joanna insisted we set up the camping table in the entry hall.

"So they can feel like they're part of the family," she said.

I agreed, though my real reason was surveillance. Colton and Simone needed adult proximity at all times. Plus, the kitchen table made a perfect buffet station. Everyone had to pick up the plates Mom had lovingly arranged and march them back to the kitchen to load up on turkey and sides. I mentally added "rethink table logistics" to next year's list.

I thought Joe should sit at the head of the table – the end closest to the kitchen – but he insisted his dad take that spot. Liam and Cami squeezed into the opposite end, closest to the kids' table. I sat between Joe and Ava, across from Mom. It was a tight fit, but no one lost circulation.

Joe's dad said grace, and just as forks began to rise, Mom tapped her glass.

"Hold on," she said. "We all need to say what we're thankful for."

Of course we did.

She went first. "I'm thankful I finally got my house set up." Then she looked at Dr. Alan. "And I'm especially thankful I have Alan in my life."

The usual answers followed: health, family, jobs. Liam mentioned his job with suspicious enthusiasm. I suspected a dig. Royce was thankful for Boys in Action. Colton and Simone were thankful for their bicycles, though I'm pretty sure Colton just copied Simone's answer. I said I was thankful to have everyone together.

Then it was Joe's turn.

"Over the years," he said, "when people asked my plans for Thanksgiving, I always told them I was going home. Home meant Mom and Dad – the place where I grew up. It was the comfortable place where people were happy to see you. From college, it was a two-and-a-half-hour drive. From my apartment in Houston, only a half-hour.

"Even after I bought this house, I didn't think of it as home. It was just a residence. A place where I slept."

He put his hand on my arm.

"That is… I didn't think of it as home until Audrey arrived. I thank God for pushing me to invite her."

I got misty-eyed. He'd never said anything like that before. I felt a little guilty that my own answer had been so generic.

Dinner buzzed with overlapping conversations – Mom and Dr. Alan telling cruise stories, which triggered Joe's parents to share their own vacation tales; Joe talking about the boys' progress in Boys in Action; and Cami bragging about Hannah's sports achievements. Royce and Hannah giggled at something over at the kids' table.

I couldn't remember the last time I'd had Thanksgiving with such a big group. Probably not since my grandmother was alive.

I looked around the table and couldn't help smiling. For the first time in ages, it felt like family.

Joe's dad asked, "So, Audrey, how did you find the funeral job?"

"The company is one of Joe's clients," I said.

"It's always nice to have an inside connection," he replied.

Then Liam jumped in, ready to deliver the world's most depressing recap of my life. "So, Joe puts you up in his house, pays your expenses, buys you a van, and now finds you a job."

Wow. When he said it out loud, I suddenly felt like a charity case on a late-night infomercial. Joe must've sensed it, because he put his hand on my thigh under the table.

"She got it on her own," Joe said, with a little attitude that made me proud.

I followed it up with, "We had lunch with his client, and they told me about it."

But Liam wasn't done. "And all you do is clean the house? Do Joe's laundry?"

He managed to suck the joy out of Thanksgiving faster than a Dyson on turbo mode. I didn't answer.

Cami leaned toward him and muttered something.

Ava, sitting between us, asked, "What was that, Cami?"

"Nothing," she said.

Unfortunately, the kids were listening. Simone, positioned directly behind Cami, piped up, "She said Mommy must be good in bed."

Silence. Absolute silence. Even the turkey stopped steaming.

I sat up straight, face burning, and began counting in my head to avoid unleashing the kind of language that would make the pilgrims blush. I finally whispered my strongest substitute curse word: "*Copenhagen.*" Only Joe heard it. He squeezed my thigh.

Simone wasn't done. "But sometimes Mommy makes a noise when she sleeps."

Joe cut in with a gravelly tone I'd never heard before. "That's not how it works around here."

Instead of taking the hint, Liam decided to go full volcano.

"I worked my butt off to get where I am. I leveraged my experience at Dad's shop to get the job at the auto parts company. Then I worked my butt off there to make manager. No one gave me a job. No one gave me a house. No one gave me a car. But my little sister gets knocked up by some Euro trash, comes home and screws all the mechanics, causes Dad to lose the shop, yet comes out like a princess!"

"*Copenhagen,*" I muttered again, louder this time.

Ava raised her eyebrows but stayed quiet.

Princess? Please. Half my wardrobe came from Goodwill. The other half from Walmart. And my van looked like it had survived a demolition derby.

Mom leaned forward, wagging her finger. "Your sister didn't cause your father to lose the shop. He lost it because he was an idiot!"

Ava added, "Kind of like you right now."

Mom turned to Dr. Alan and Joe's parents. "Bill let his emotions get in the way of his decisions. He made a lot of foolish mistakes."

Liam stood up and stormed off. A moment later, the door to the driveway slammed hard enough to rattle the windows.

Cami stood. "Come on, Hannah."

Joanna intercepted her. "Cami, why don't you help us clear the table before you go?"

Cami opened her mouth, probably to deliver a dramatic monologue, but settled for a sigh. She grabbed plates from the kids' table and marched them to the kitchen. Joanna followed with her own stack, taking the shorter route behind Joe's dad.

Joanna acted as if nothing had happened. I heard her say to Cami, "Audrey did a lovely job with the Christmas decorations, don't you think?"

"Vintage," Cami replied.

"I was thinking cozy," Joanna said. "I understand they're from your mother-in-law's house."

I had to hand it to Joanna; she was trying to de-escalate the nuclear fallout with the grace of a seasoned diplomat. Cami didn't respond.

Most of the group drifted to the living room. Joe's dad went through the kitchen. Joe and Ava stayed with me in the dining room.

Joe put a hand on my shoulder. "Should I go after Liam?"

"Why?" I asked. "To beat the *Spitsbergen* out of him?"

He snorted, then tried to hide his smile when I winced. "Sorry. Your Nordic cuss words still sound funny. I'll let Liam take care of himself."

In the kitchen, Joanna asked, "Have you and Liam ever hosted Thanksgiving?"

I knew the answer. They had never hosted anything. Not Thanksgiving, not Easter, not even a backyard barbecue.

"No," Cami said, confused why the interrogation continued.

"Oh," Joanna said sweetly. "Well, I'm sure your turn will come. Maybe Audrey can give you some tips."

I suddenly realized I had underestimated Joe's mom. With one innocent-sounding question, she managed to highlight that my "successful" brother and sister-in-law had never stepped up, while I, the family disaster, had somehow pulled off Thanksgiving for a crowd.

I might not have money or status, but for once, I had something better. I had the right people in my corner.

CHAPTER 61

Joe

Had I gone after Liam, the results probably wouldn't have looked good for either of us. I may not have been able to beat the *Spitzbergen* out of him, but if he made any further derogatory comments about Audrey, I might have tried. I probably had a better chance against him now than I did back in school when he was in better shape.

Audrey went to her bedroom, and Beverly followed after her and closed the door. I started to follow, too, but Ava stopped me in the hallway.

"Give them a few minutes," she said. Then she asked, "*Spitsbergen?*"

I merely replied, "Yeah."

"And it sounded like she said *Copenhagen* at her brother's tirade."

"It's an Audrey thing," I said. "It's more about her tone of voice than the actual word."

Ava surprised me with, "Her brother is such an *Oslo!*"

I snickered at her observation. That was the same word Audrey uses for drivers who cut us off or wouldn't let us merge into their lane.

Ava and I leaned against the wall on either side of the door, pretending we weren't eavesdropping.

"Honey, don't let Liam get to you," Beverly said. "He's forgotten how much help he got over the years. Your father got him that job. Or at least was instrumental in him getting it. Citadel Auto Parts was our supplier for years, and your dad had a good relationship with the local operations manager. He called the guy and put in a good word for Liam.

"I'm also disappointed Cami didn't call him out about the house. Her parents helped them with the down payment."

"*Oslo*," Ava whispered again.

"He's been one as long as I've known him," I whispered back.

Audrey responded, "Yeah, well, he's right about the mechanics and me. I already regret it. He doesn't need to rub my face in it."

"We got Colton out of it, and that's a good thing," Beverly reminded.

* * *

Sunday, Griffin came over. I stood on the ladder next to the house while he held up a string of white Christmas lights.

"You're really into this whole domesticated man thing," he commented.

"You mean, being a responsible homeowner and active member of the community?" I asked.

"Is that what this is?" he asked in return.

I came down to reposition the ladder.

"Anything more with that Starbucks girl you were flirting with?" I asked.

The last time we talked, he mentioned running into the same girl at Starbucks several mornings a week.

"Noriko," he said. "Yeah. I'm taking her to Costa Rica for New Year's."

With the ladder moved three feet to the right, I climbed back up.

"How did you jump from flirting at a coffee shop to taking a trip together?" I asked.

He handed me the electric drill and box of hanging hooks as he said, "Maybe if your prison mama let you out more, you'd know."

Prison mama. Jailhouse babe. Nose ring girl. My favorite was trauma drama baby mama. Griffin had several terms for Audrey, none of which were flattering. Some of which were raunchy. They don't seem as funny now as they did a few months ago.

"You know, there's more to her than just her prison time," I said. "But I've been busy lately. Especially when she was away, and I looked after the kids."

He clicked his tongue and shook his head before continuing his story. "Usually, when I saw Noriko, we were both standing in line. After a few times, I would try to get there a little early and wait for her, then act as if I'd just gotten there."

I cleared my throat and said, "Simp," before using the electric drill to screw in another hook.

"Think what you want, but she's into me, too," he defended.

I hooked the hanging strand of lights into the newly attached hook and prepared to install the next one. "So, how'd you go from coffee shop stalker to dating?"

"Usually, we would chat in line, but after we got our coffee, we would go our separate ways. But one day, I came in, and she was already there, sitting at a table with her coffee. We started talking, and before I knew it, we were both an hour late for work. I got her number, and before we left the shop, we set up a date for that Saturday."

"And now it's serious?" I asked.

"Working on it," he said.

He noticed I had reached the end of the strand of lights and grabbed a box of lights from the stack by the front door.

"Tell me about her," I said as he pulled the lights from the box. "What do you like about her?"

He removed the wire twist tie that held the lights in a tight little bundle and then shook the strand loose.

"Oh, you know I'm easy," he said. "No tattoos, no piercings, no kids, and no jail time."

I snorted and said, "So, she's the anti-Audrey."

He shrugged. "She cooks. But mostly Japanese stuff. And did I mention she's into me?"

"Yeah. I'm still wondering about that," I said, taking the strand from Griffin. "Costa Rica, huh?"

"Yeah! The weather's great, even in late December. They say the beaches on the Pacific side are good at that time of year. It's a good excuse to see her in a swimsuit." He paused as if he had just found a flaw in his logic. "Not that I need to see her in a swimsuit. I've already seen her in her birthday suit."

"Of course you have," I noted.

He ignored my sarcasm and asked, "Your firm still has the whole week off between Christmas and New Year's, doesn't it?"

"Yep. Mandatory vacation," I said.

"So, where are you going?"

"It's a bit of a challenge to find kid-friendly places in the winter that won't break the bank," I said. "There's a place on the way to Galveston I've been looking into. Black Bear Lodge. It's kid-friendly and has an indoor water park."

Griffin stared at me for a moment. "Kid-friendly? Bro, you're not even sleeping with the woman. Or has that changed?"

"No. Still separate bedrooms."

"But you're making plans as if you're…." his voice trailed off. He looked around the lawn, then leaned in and whispered, "Are you okay? Do we need to stage an intervention?"

* * *

The street preacher must have made his circuit again because he was back at the corner I had to pass on the way to my car.

"The master says, Look, Joe Plumber, Look, Joe Farmer…." He pointed directly at me and added, "Joe Accountant. I gave them to you to take care of. Do me proud."

I had no idea what he was talking about, but I slowed my pace to hear what came next out of his mouth.

"'Cause when he comes back to see what you've done with who he's given you, you want to hear him say, 'Well done!'"

Only when I reached my car did I realize the preacher had said, '*who* he's given you,' not '*what* he's given you.'

CHAPTER 62

Audrey

When Joe got home from work, he announced he had "two things" to tell me, wearing the grin of a man who knew he was about to drop a bombshell and was enjoying every second of it.

"You want me to go with you to your office Christmas party?" I asked, making sure I hadn't misheard.

"Yeah. It'll be like another date. Just us, no kids."

Just us… and several hundred of his coworkers who probably have framed diplomas, monogrammed briefcases, and the ability to drink wine without leaving fingerprints on the glass.

I pointed at two plates of meatloaf, mashed potatoes, and green beans. "Take those to the table for Colton and Simone."

"Yeah, sorry I forgot to mention the party earlier," he said. "I RSVP'd before you got out, and then I got distracted with other things."

Translation: I was probably the "other things," and his coworkers have definitely discussed me over lunch. George alone could fill an entire break room with stories.

"It'll be fun," he said. "Dinner, drinks, dancing."

I followed him with two more plates – one for Royce and one for me. "And stares and whispers," I added, heading back for the last plate.

"You already know Debbie," he said. "We can sit with her and her husband."

True. At least I wouldn't be walking into a corporate lion's den without a familiar face.

"What's the dress code?" I asked.

He hesitated. "Formal."

"As in tuxedos and evening gowns?"

"Well… some of the partners wear tuxedos. Most guys just wear suits. Just wear something nice."

That was a problem. "I don't have formal," I said. "And my nicest clothes are… not that."

"What are y'all talking about?" Royce asked.

"Joe wants me to go with him to his company party, where all the women will wear fancy dresses," I said.

"Like Cinderella?" Simone asked.

I said, "Yes," at the exact moment Joe said, "No."

"It's not that kind of fancy," he tried to explain. Simone stared at him with the blank confusion of someone who believes all fancy is ball-gown fancy.

"It's still fancier than anything I own," I said.

"I want you to come with me," he told me. "Use the debit card if you need to get something."

"The one for groceries and gas?" I asked.

"Yeah. Buy a dress. Just be reasonable."

Reasonable. In other words: please don't come home with a sequined ball gown that costs more than the van.

Tempting, though.

CHAPTER 63

Joe

Audrey and I both forgot that I had a second announcement until later that evening. When she got out of the shower, I was waiting for her, sitting on the side of my bed nearest her vanity area.

"Did I mention my office is closed between Christmas and New Year's Day?" I asked.

"No," she said. "What does that mean?"

"It means everyone takes a vacation at the same time."

I smiled broadly, hoping she took the hint of what that meant.

"And…?" she asked with less enthusiasm than I expected. She didn't get the hint.

"Have you heard of Black Bear Lodge in League City?"

She wrapped her hair in a towel as I described the hotel, built to look like a mountain lodge.

"A mountain lodge sounds a little out of place for this area," she pointed out.

"But that's the charm. Something we don't usually see around here. And it has an indoor water park."

"So, you're having a guys' getaway?" she asked.

I couldn't believe she still didn't get it. I picked up the laptop next to me on the bed and patted the spot on the bed to my left. At least she took *that* hint and sat down by me. I angled the laptop so she could see the screen, then touched the image to start a video. There it was, the mountain lodge with log beams and a giant fireplace in the lobby. The scene quickly transitioned to the waterpark. A smiling family stood in swimsuits under a waterfall, with waterslides visible behind them.

"The kids will love it," I told her.

"What?"

"You don't have plans for that week, do you?" I asked, knowing full well she didn't.

She had a blank look on her face, like her brain short-circuited and needed to reboot.

Her answer came out in a whisper. "No."

"Good!" I said, trying to exude enough energy to make up for her lack of enthusiasm. "Because I booked us for three nights. That gives us three days at the waterpark. Or if we get tired of that, the Kemah Boardwalk and Galveston's Moody Gardens are close by."

"You booked us rooms at this lodge?"

"Yeah," I said, surprised that she hadn't fully grasped it. "I got us a family suite. It has a room with bunk beds for the kids and a regular bed in the main room."

Her face finally brightened as the lightbulb in her head finally came on. "You're taking us on a vacation?"

"Yeah," I confirmed. "Your mother said the kids had never been on vacation, and I figured that meant you haven't had one in a while either."

She leaned into me to watch the video that continued to play in a loop. When she'd seen the whole thing again, she planted a kiss on my cheek.

"Does that mean you approve?" I asked.

She nodded. "So,.. um… We'll finally be sharing a bed?"

"The room has a sofa that pulls out into a bed. I can take that," I said.

"Or," she said, "we could just share the bed."

I rested my hand on her leg and told her in a low voice, "When we were teenagers, it was hard keeping my hands off you, even when

I knew your parents were in the next room. Lying next to you in bed, I don't know if I could control myself."

"Maybe you shouldn't have to," she said.

I glanced toward the bathroom. I was going to need a cold shower.

"You know I'm traditional," I said. "We should be married before sleeping together."

"There's that proposal again," she teased.

I removed my hand from her thigh and slid the laptop closer onto my lap to hide my…uh… interest. I finally said, "I really need to watch how I phrase things."

We decided we would wait until Christmas to tell the kids.

CHAPTER 64

Audrey

Joe finished getting ready and wandered over to my vanity area, clearly performing a full inspection. He watched me finish my makeup and clip on the pearl-drop earrings I'd found at T.J. Maxx during Tuesday's emergency "find heels or die trying" mission. The earring fittings were gold, the shoes were glittery silver, and together they made me look like a confused Christmas ornament. But no one would be staring at my ears and feet simultaneously unless they were very bored.

I'd hoped for strappy heels, but the pumps would do. Simone had declared them "Cinderella slippers," which was her review for every single item we looked at that day. Shoes? Cinderella. Dresses? Cinderella. A random blue spatula? Cinderella.

"Stop staring," I told Joe. "You're making me nervous."

"Why? You look fantastic."

"You clean up pretty well, too," I said. He wore a dark suit with a red tie so bright it could guide ships through fog.

I checked myself in the mirror again. "I look like a lost bridesmaid."

"No one will think that."

He was adorable, but also wrong. Women would absolutely recognize the satin A-line boat-neck baby-blue dress as a bridesmaid survivor. Goodwill had an entire rack of dresses abandoned by bridal parties who no longer speak to each other. And if the designs didn't give them away, the fact that they hung next to donated wedding gowns sealed the deal. Simone called them princess dresses. Especially the wedding gowns.

Still, the dress was pretty, and only $16. A bargain for something worn once and then emotionally discarded. Simone approved, though she wished it were "fluffier," which I'm pretty sure meant "please add a hoop skirt, Mommy." A silent reference to Cinderella, I'm sure.

"You can tell people I wandered in from the wedding reception next door," I told Joe.

"Yeah, because accountants are a much more exciting crowd than a wedding party," he said.

I covered up with Mom's white wool overcoat before we left.

* * *

The valet lane at the Hyatt Regency was a full-blown traffic jam. We inched forward for five solid minutes before finally reaching the entrance. The instant Joe put the Camry in park, valets descended on us like we were A-list celebrities—or like the BMW behind us had somewhere far more important to be.

Before I could open my door, Joe caught my left hand.

"Wait," he said. "You're missing an accessory."

My glittery clutch sat in my lap. Earrings? Present. Bracelet? Skipped on purpose.

"What are you talking about?" I asked.

Joe ignored the valet at his window, who was now clearing his throat with the urgency of a man about to perform the Heimlich. Joe slid a ring onto my fourth finger. A ring I had never seen before in my life.

"Joe, what is this?"

He let go of my hand and stepped out of the car without answering. I scrambled out after him, clutch clutched, silently praying the person driving away in the Camry was a valet and not a polite thief.

Hotel staff waved us out of the driveway. I held up my newly adorned hand. "Joe. What is this?"

He grinned. "What does it look like?"

I tilted my hand under the lights. "Is it real?"

"It's a real diamond in a real white-gold setting."

"That's not what I meant. It looks like an engagement ring."

"Well," he said, "you did claim I proposed. Twice. And if memory serves, you accepted both times."

People streamed past, blissfully unaware that my entire life had just spun on its axis. Joe and I stared at each other, wearing identical *now what* faces.

As if my previous answers – and my ridiculous grin – weren't enough, he asked, properly this time, "Will you marry me?"

I rested my ringed hand on his arm. "Joe, we've never even had a proper kiss."

He slid his hands around my waist and pulled me in for a kiss before I could finish breathing. I wrapped my arms around his neck, holding on like he might change his mind if I let go. The cold disappeared. My brain fizzed. My knees forgot their job description.

Then Debbie materialized, placed her hands on our shoulders, and said, "Kisses are just as sweet inside where it's warm."

I giggled and let her steer us toward the entrance. Halfway to the restroom – where my mascara was about to face its greatest challenge – I remembered I hadn't actually answered the latest proposal.

"Yes!" I blurted, startling a nearby couple. That made three acceptances, if anyone was keeping score.

Before I disappeared into the restroom, we exchanged "I love you"s with the intensity of people being separated by international borders.

With Joe, obviously. Not Debbie. Debbie and I are nowhere near that level.

CHAPTER 65

Joe

My old fiancée Mindy would have dropped five hundred bucks on a dress without batting an eye. Not my money, thank goodness, but still more than my comfort level. Audrey could have spent a couple of hundred before I questioned it. She wouldn't tell me how much her new dress cost, but I checked the debit card records for the day she bought it and found she'd spent less than a hundred dollars among two discount stores and a charity thrift shop. And the thrift-shop dress she showed me looked perfect. The next day, I visited a jewelry store.

* * *

At the valet station, I was lost in Audrey until Debbie's interruption startled me. Apparently, she'd been standing there for some time before deciding we needed to move inside. I felt flushed as if caught doing something naughty. Not that I cared as others passed by, but only because it was Debbie, my office mom. Her husband stood behind her with an apologetic smile.

"I told her not to bother you," he said.

Debbie handed Audrey a tissue and touched the corner of her right eye, saying, "You may need to fix that."

"Thank you," Audrey said with a giggle.

The four of us walked into the lobby as Audrey dabbed the tissue on her cheeks with her right hand while staring at the ring on her left.

She would have stumbled into signs, columns, and other partygoers had I not been guiding her through the building.

Debbie leaned her head to Audrey and whispered, "That way," pointing to the restroom sign posted next to a hallway.

"Thank you," Audrey said.

Then she grabbed my hand and said, "I love you."

I snuck in another kiss before saying it back.

* * *

That next Monday morning, the street preacher started early. I usually only see him at lunchtime or in the evenings.

He waved his hands at the passersby to punctuate his message. As I approached close enough to hear his words, I saw him point at the sky, saying, "The Master said…." Then, when I was directly across from him, he pointed at me and continued, "Well done, my good and faithful servant."

It sounded like he recycled one of his old sermons. I just nodded and kept walking.

CHAPTER 66

Joe

I lay in that odd state of awareness where I sensed the sun was up without opening my eyes. Aware enough to hear the bed in the kids' bunk room creak from someone climbing down the ladder from the top bunk. Colton. Since Royce had the upper bunk at home, Colton insisted he get the upper bunk on vacation.

Last night, Royce warned us, "If he falls off, don't blame me."

Audrey and I acknowledged the warning and let Colton take the top anyway.

After the creaking, I heard Royce whisper, "Where are you going?"

Colton whispered back, "To see if it's morning yet."

The bunkroom didn't have a window, only a nightlight below a picture of bear cubs playing by a stream. I opened an eye to confirm the main room was a tad brighter than when we went to bed last night. Enough sunlight snuck in between the panels of the closed curtains to let me see Colton peeking from around the corner when I gently moved Audrey's hair out of my face. We locked eyes, and he ducked back to the bunk room.

"It's light outside," he reported back to his siblings. "Joe's awake, but Momma's still asleep."

Then I heard Simone join the conversation. "They're probably tired because they were exercising last night. I heard them."

Dang! We thought they were asleep!

Epilogue

Audrey

Royce and Livvy sat on the rug in the living room, hunched over Mom's photo album on the coffee table. Royce called it "Nana's picture book," even though Nana made only a cameo appearance. It was our wedding album. Mom had taken the photos we snapped that day and sent them off to some magical company that turns chaos into hardcover keepsakes.

I sat at the kitchen table, folding laundry, pretending not to monitor them while absolutely monitoring them.

"I took most of these pictures," Royce told Livvy with the confidence of a seasoned professional. "But sometimes they got strangers to take some so I could be in the picture, too."

Livvy leaned in. "Maybe you can be a photographer when you grow up."

"I'm already a photographer," he said, deeply offended.

"I mean, for a job," she clarified, gently crushing his dreams.

The album cover showed Joe and me in our wedding outfits in front of the giant mall Christmas tree.

"That's the same picture on the wall," Royce said, pointing to the spot where my campout picture used to hang before it was replaced by "Look, Momma accidentally got married."

"Her dress is pretty," Livvy said.

"Simone helped her pick it out at Goodwill," Royce announced. "It looks like a curtain."

"It does NOT look like a curtain," Livvy snapped, as if he'd insulted *her* personally. "You don't know anything about dresses."

She wasn't wrong. Royce's fashion expertise peaked at "clean" and "not itchy." The dress did have layers that could resemble curtains to the untrained eye, but I preferred to think of it as a tiered Christmas tree. Joe wore a black suit he already owned and a bow tie I bought at the mall for $12.99.

Royce flipped to the first page. "This is when we were about to leave the house. Joe carried Momma to put her in the van. Simone calls him Daddy now, but I keep forgetting."

Livvy pointed to another picture. "Who's he?"

Without looking, I knew exactly which one she meant: the gray-haired man in the green sweater.

"That's Mr. Walter, the preacher," Royce said. "He had to sign the marriage paper."

Reverend Walter Jacobson, the funeral home chaplain, had refused to sign our license at the funeral home. "Under no circumstances," he'd said… before suggesting we meet at the mall. Because nothing says holy matrimony like the food court.

Royce flipped ahead. "The best thing about the mall was… Santa Claus!"

I pictured it: Simone on Santa's lap, Royce and Colton on one side, Joe and me on the other, all of us smiling like we hadn't just sprinted through Dillard's to get there.

"One of the workers took that picture," Royce said. "That was after we told Santa what we wanted for Christmas."

Livvy kept flipping until she stopped at a picture of Joe's parents. "Who are they?"

"They're Joma and Mr. Steve," Royce said. "Joma had her mouth open like this—" He made a face I couldn't see but desperately wished I could. "'Cause she couldn't believe they got married. And Mr. Steve looked like this—" Another face I missed. "'Cause he didn't understand why they wore wedding clothes."

Livvy gasped. "Your mom didn't invite them to the wedding?"

"They didn't invite anyone," Royce said proudly. "They didn't even tell anyone. They only told us that morning. We got to skip school."

"You're so lucky!"

"We went to my Nana's house, too," he said, flipping to the next page. "It's new. And super small. When she saw Momma and Joe in their wedding clothes, she screamed and did this—"

I stood up to see. Royce pressed his hands to his cheeks, mouth wide open, full Kevin McAllister.

"It was a happy scream," he said. "She came over and spent the night with us so Joe and Momma could go to a hotel to practice being married."

Livvy blinked. "How do you practice being married?"

"Don't ask me," Royce said, shutting that down immediately.

I ducked back into the kitchen before anyone decided to ask *me*.

Acknowledgment

I want to thank Gordon Rottman, Terry Miller, Stan Marshall, and Linda Bromley for their advice on early drafts.

I thank Beverly Rosenbaum for her insightful editing recommendations that made the story flow better. I thank Ruth M., Allison G. and Michael G. for their constructive feedback on what I thought at the time was a finished manuscript.

About the Author

Todd H. Davis is the father of three kids (two girls and a boy) who are now in their early twenties. He lives with his "smarter-than-me" wife in the Houston, Texas, suburb of Cypress, which is the setting for several of his novels.

Todd spent most of his life in the Houston area, except for the two years in Japan in his twenties, teaching English in churches in the Nagasaki area. While he was getting used to Asian culture, his wife, who had recently arrived in the US from China for studies, was getting used to American culture. They have spent the years since then getting used to each other.

He has self-published eight books through Amazon KDP, most of them about chosen family.

The Trailer Behind the Garage
The Gas Station Girl
The Lingering Scent of Wrong Assumptions
The DollarFly Girls
The Kennedi Identity
Robin and the Rednecks
Sunny's House
From Coffee to Chaos

You can contact him through his website:
www.toddhdavis.com

Books by Todd H. Davis

The Trailer Behind the Garage (Book 1)

Can the Jensen kids make it on their own after their parents' deaths? When older sibling Sophie becomes the family leader upon turning 17, the family experiences a variety of life events – at times funny, sweet, and challenging – as they figure out how to be a family without parents, even if it means including an outsider; and maybe a little romance along the way.

The Gas Station Girl (Book 2)

When 16-year-old John finds an incoherent young woman stumbling around a gas station late at night trying to get into cars with strangers, the advice from his older sister Sophie is to open his car door. If the young woman gets in, bring her home. She gets in. Alia, the 17-year-old sex trafficking victim finds a new life with the help of John's family.

The Lingering Scent (Book 3)

Emi catches feelings for her best friend Annie's fake boyfriend Joel; however, dethroned queen bee Sienna's jealousy leads to a plan to break up Annie and Joel. Alia, a former runaway who lives with Emi, suspects something is amiss with Sienna. With reputations at stake, can the friends work together to expose the truth before it's too late?

The DollarFly Girls (Prequel to Gas Station Girl)

When Alia ran away from an abusive father, she thought her online friend was taking her to an informal group home where the teens who lived there worked odd jobs to pay the bills. She didn't know that meant nights with men at cheap motels. Her first escape attempt failed, but months later a new girl inspires her to try again.

The Kennedi Identity (Book 4)

At fifteen, Kennedi gives birth alone in a Texas gas station after escaping a sex trafficking ring. Placed in foster care with her newborn, DNA tests uncover buried truths and spark a custody fight. As adults argue her future, Kennedi must choose what family really means.

Robin and the Rednecks

A young wannabe social media influencer reluctantly hitches a ride with a country boy and his kinfolk to avoid the police. Once over the initial shock of her boyfriend's crime, fear of arrest is replaced by fear of strangers taking her to who knows where. But her affection for the group grows as she helps them renovate a remote cabin in West Texas.

Sunny's House

Abandoned, pregnant, and haunted by her past, Mary Kate finds an unlikely refuge with a dying woman and her grieving husband. As healing turns to love, whispers of scandal threaten the fragile family they've built. *Sunny's House* is a story of redemption, resilience, and unexpected belonging.

From Coffee to Chaos

What starts as the world's worst coffee date turns into bunk beds, parenting classes, campouts, and chaos. But somewhere between jail visits and Christmas lights, Joe discovers that love—and family—can sneak up when you least expect it.